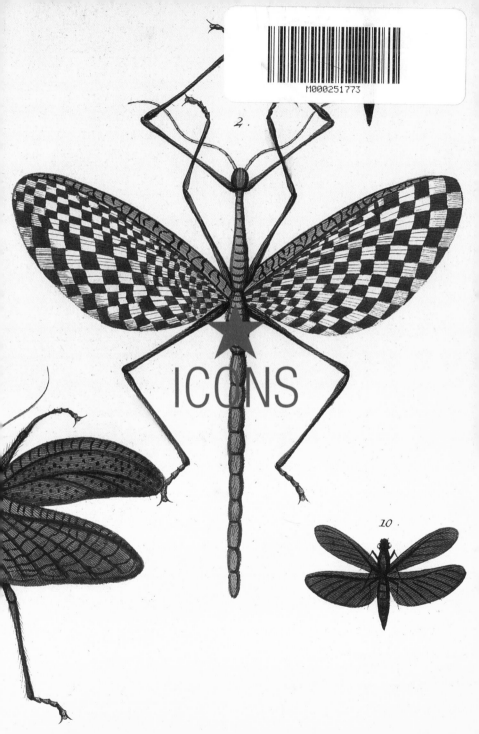

2.

10.

ALBERTUS SEBA

Butterflies
&
Insects

*And there are no other
collections in all of Europe
wherein so many rare pieces
are to be found*

ALBERTUS SEBA

6.

11.

COVER
Butterflies and silkmoths from South-East Asia to Australia

ENDPAPERS
1-2 Walking stick 5 Katydid 9-10 Dragonflies

PAGES 2–3
Tropical butterflies distributed worldwide and caddis flies

PAGES 4–5
Butterflies and silkmoths from South-East Asia to Australia

PAGES 10–11
Butterflies and hawkmoths from Europe and
tropical Central and South America

PAGES 14–15
Butterflies from South America and Africa and
moths from Malay Archipelago, New Guinea and America

PAGES 18–19
3 Katydid 4-7 Praying mantids

© 2004 TASCHEN GmbH
Hohenzollernring 53, D–50672 Köln
www.taschen.com

Edited by Petra Lamers-Schütze, Cologne
Design by Claudia Frey, Cologne
Production by Ute Wachendorf, Cologne

Captions by Klaus-Dieter Bierwirth, Sven Bradler, Thomas Hörnschemeyer,
Sonja Wedmann, Francisco Welter-Schultes, Rainer Willmann

English translation: Anne Hentschell (introduction),
Malcolm Green (captions)
French translation: Anne Charrière (introduction),
Bernard Landry and Hélène Trudel (captions)
Spanish translation: José García

Printed in Italy
ISBN 3–8228–2431–3

ALBERTUS SEBA

Butterflies & Insects

Schmetterlinge & Insekten · Papillons & Insectes
Mariposas & Insectos

TASCHEN

KÖLN LONDON LOS ANGELES MADRID PARIS TOKYO

8

ALBERTUS SEBA'S *collection of natural specimens and its* PICTORIAL COLLECTION

IRMGARD MÜSCH

By becoming an apothecary, Albertus Seba, who was born in 1665 in the East Frisian town of Etzel, chose a profession with close ties to natural history. Unlike today, medications were not synthetically made but mixed together from natural constituents. A whole range of traditional recipes were available to those versed in the art of creating remedies from animal, vegetable and mineral ingredients. But many did not stop there. They continued the search for new methods, collecting natural specimens from distant lands, studying them, and testing their potential uses. Their passion for collecting and researching often extended beyond immediate pharmaceutical applications. In many instances apothecaries started major natural history collections and contributed personally to the growing knowledge of nature.

With his "Die Deutsche Apotheke" (German Apothecary's Shop), as he called his business, Seba rapidly earned an excellent reputation for himself. Financially, too, he was successful – something which would enable him to establish his comprehensive collection of natural specimens. Not relying solely on casual customers who happened to pass by his apothecary, Seba actively sought them out. He traded in drugs from overseas, advertising his prices in an Amsterdam newspaper. He supplied departing ships with cases of medicines and treated their crews. It is related how, whenever a ship arrived in port, Seba would hasten down to the harbour without delay and administer his medicines to the exhausted sailors. Any natural specimens that they had brought with them he would then be able to purchase at a good price or accept in exchange for his medications.

In Amsterdam, Seba was ideally situated for starting such a collection of natural curios and he succeeded in assembling a wealth of natural specimens whose fame spread beyond the bounds of Amsterdam.

ALBERTUS SEBA'S THESAURUS

On 30 October 1731 a contract was signed in Amsterdam between three parties: Seba and the agents of two publishing houses agreed to produce a major work of 400 plates depicting Seba's collection. Ultimately, the Thesaurus incorporated a magnificent 446 plates, 175 of them double-page. The four volumes appeared over a span of 30 years, from 1734–1765. The commentary on the plates was published in a Latin-French and a Latin-Dutch edition, so as to reach a broad international readership of natural historians, collectors and book lovers. Seba wrote the text for the first two volumes largely himself, but also had other naturalists assist him. Volume I of the

Thesaurus opens with a few pages devoted to illustrations of the plant skeletons that Seba had prepared and conserved using his own special technique. These are followed by depictions of plants and animals from South America and Asia. Alongside lizards, birds, frogs, spiders and other creatures, Seba includes a few fantastical creatures, such as dragons. Volume II is dedicated primarily to snakes, but a few plants and other animals are also depicted on the plates for decorative purposes and in order to illustrate the reptiles' environment. Volume III is devoted to marine life. The imposing variety of sea creatures includes scallops, starfish, squid, sea urchins and fish. Volume IV presents, in nearly 100 plates, a large collection of insects followed by a few pages of minerals and fossils from Seba's cabinet.

Publication of a work like the Thesaurus called for considerable sums of money. Hugely expensive to produce were above all the many illustration plates, whose engraving was a laborious and drawn-out task. The names of no less than 13 artists are recorded as being employed on the transferral of the drawings, frontispiece, and portrait to the copperplates. The expensive work was initially published in black-and-white. It is not known whether the publishers also offered a hand-painted edition, which would naturally have raised the price and profit margin considerably. Buyers probably had the work painted at their own extra expense by specialist colourists. The gorgeous colours add substantially to the attractiveness of the plates, but their purpose was not just aesthetic enhancement. They had a scientific use as well. Some specimens, such as those of butterflies, snakes and shellfish, are only distinguishable by their colouring, and the differences in patterning of many fauna can barely be discerned in black-and-white. Whether or not originally in colour, whether or not based on existing illustrations, the Thesaurus remains an impressive example of a Baroque book. The illustrations in the second, third and fourth volumes, which rely much less on previously published sources, increasingly follow contemporary conventions in scientific literature. For best possible visual clarity, the animals are portrayed without any overlapping and with their size ratios correct – albeit in mirror image, which in the case of snail shells spiralling counter-clockwise became the source of some confusion. What was retained, though, was an ornamental arrangement of the objects on the plates, which is demonstrated by the symmetrically arranged snake plates as well as by artistically arranged shells and insects. Just as with the collection, there were thus always two aspects to the illustrations: they served both scientific instruction and aesthetic appreciation.

The Thesaurus treated an important collection of natural specimens of the early 18th century. As a book, the actual stationary collection became mobile and permanently accessible to many interested persons – even when the collection itself had long been scattered to the four winds.

This publication presents a representative selection of the most beautiful butterflies and insects from the fourth volume of the complete edition.

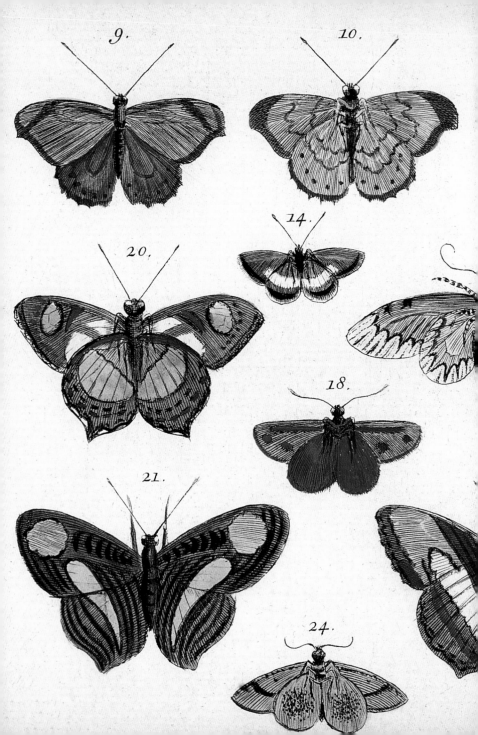

ALBERTUS SEBA'S *Naturaliensammlung* *und ihr* BILDINVENTAR

IRMGARD MÜSCH

Albertus Seba, 1665 im ostfriesischen Etzel geboren, wählte mit dem Apothekerberuf eine Profession, die zu seiner Zeit eng mit naturhistorischen Studien verknüpft war. Medikamente wurden nicht wie heute synthetisch hergestellt, sondern aus natürlichen Bestandteilen gemischt. Um aus Tieren, Pflanzen und Mineralien Heilmittel zu gewinnen, stand Arzneikundigen eine ganze Reihe überlieferter Rezepte zur Verfügung. Viele suchten jedoch nach neuen Wegen, sammelten Naturalien aus allen Himmelsrichtungen, studierten sie und erprobten ihre mögliche Verwendbarkeit. Vielfach verselbstständigte sich die Sammel- und Forscherleidenschaft über einen unmittelbaren pharmazeutischen Nutzen hinaus. Mehrfach legten Apotheker bedeutende naturhistorische Sammlungen an und trugen selbst zur wachsenden Kenntnis der Natur bei.

Mit seinem Geschäft, das er „Die deutsche Apotheke" nannte, erwarb sich Seba rasch einen guten Ruf. Zu dem großen finanziellen Erfolg seiner Apotheke, der ihm das Anlegen seiner umfangreichen Naturaliensammlung ermöglichte, trug ganz wesentlich bei, dass sich der geschäftstüchtige Seba nicht nur auf Laufkundschaft verließ. Vielmehr handelte er auch mit pharmazeutischen Rohstoffen (Drogen) aus Übersee, für die er unter Angabe der Preise in einer Amsterdamer Zeitung warb. Außerdem lieferte er den auslaufenden Schiffen Reiseapotheken und behandelte die Seeleute. Der Überlieferung zufolge eilte Seba unverzüglich auf die in den Hafen einlaufenden Schiffe und behandelte die Matrosen mit seinen Arzneien. Dabei gelang es ihm, den erschöpften Männern Naturalien, die sie mitgebracht hatten, günstig abzukaufen oder gegen Medikamente einzutauschen.

Mit Amsterdam hatte sich Seba einen Standort für den Aufbau einer Naturaliensammlung ausgesucht, wie er ihn besser kaum hätte finden können und es gelang ihm, eine bedeutende Sammlung aufzubauen, deren Ruf über die Grenzen Amsterdams hinausging.

DER THESAURUS VON ALBERTUS SEBA

Am 30. Oktober 1731 schlossen in Amsterdam drei Parteien einen Vertrag: Vertreter zweier Verlage und Seba vereinbarten darin, das Kabinett des Sammlers in einem großen Werk mit etwa 400 Tafeln zu publizieren. Tatsächlich umfasst der Thesaurus stolze 446 Tafeln, davon 175 als Doppelseite. Die vier Bände erschienen in einem Zeitraum von 30 Jahren, von 1734–1765. Die begleitenden Erläuterungen zu den Tafeln wurden jeweils in einer lateinisch-französischen und einer lateinisch-niederländischen Fassung veröffentlicht, da sich Seba mit dem Thesaurus an ein internationales Publikum von Naturforschern, Sammlern und Buchliebhabern wandte. Den Text der ersten beiden Bände verfasste Seba weitgehend selbst, doch ließ er sich von anderen Naturforschern unterstützen. Am Anfang des ersten Thesaurus-Bandes stehen zunächst einige Seiten mit Abbildungen von Pflanzenskeletten, die Seba mit seiner speziellen Präparationstechnik bearbeitet und konserviert hatte. Dann folgen Darstellungen von Tieren und Pflanzen aus dem südamerikanischen und asiatischen Raum. Neben Eidechsen, Vögeln, Fröschen, Spinnen und anderen Tieren finden sich auch einige Fabelwesen wie Drachen. Band II gilt vorrangig den Schlangen, zu dekorativen Zwecken und zur Veranschaulichung der Lebensweise der Reptilien sind allerdings auch einige Pflanzen und andere Tiere auf den Tafeln zu sehen. Dem maritimen Lebensraum ist der dritte Band gewidmet: Es erwartet den Betrachter eine überwältigende Vielzahl von Meerestieren wie Muscheln, Seesterne, Tintenfische, Seeigel und Fische. Der abschließende Band präsentiert auf knapp 100 Tafeln eine umfangreiche Sammlung von Insekten, gefolgt von einigen Seiten mit Darstellungen der Mineralien und Fossilien aus Sebas Kabinett.

Das Unterfangen, ein Werk wie den Thesaurus herauszugeben, erforderte beträchtlichen Einsatz von Geldmitteln. Vor allem die vielen Bildtafeln, deren Anfertigung mit hohem Zeitaufwand verbunden war, verursachten immense Kosten. Allein 13 Künstler, die Tafeln, Frontispiz und Porträt auf Druckplatten übertrugen, sind namentlich bekannt. Das teure Werk erschien zunächst in schwarz-weißer Ausführung. Es ist nicht bekannt, ob auch die Verlage selbst eine kolorierte Ausgabe anboten, die den Preis und die Gewinnspanne natürlich erheblich gesteigert hätte. Vermutlich ließen die Käufer das Werk auf eigene Rechnung farblich fassen und wandten sich dazu an spezialisierte Koloristen. Die Farbenpracht der Tafeln ist ein besonderer Genuss, doch erhöhte die Kolorierung nicht nur den ästhetischen Reiz, sondern auch den wissenschaftlichen Nutzen. Beispielsweise lassen sich manche Exemplare von Schmetterlingen, Schlangen oder Muscheln nur mit Hilfe der Farbe unterscheiden, während in Schwarz-Weiß die Unterschiede in der Musterung mancher Tiere kaum auszumachen sind. Mit oder ohne Kolorierung überzeugt der Thesaurus in jedem Fall als ein beeindruckendes Beispiel barocker Buchkunst. Die Tafeln des zweiten bis vierten Bandes entsprechen zunehmend einer zeitüblichen wissenschaftlichen Präsentation. Die Tiere sind – fein säuberlich nach Gattungen getrennt – aufgereiht. Für eine größtmögliche Lesbarkeit der Abbildungen sind die Tiere ohne Überschneidungen und mit einheitlichem Größenmaßstab abgebildet – allerdings seitenverkehrt, was bei Schnecken mit linksdrehendem Gehäuse zu Missverständnissen führte. Erhalten blieb eine ornamentale Anordnung der Objekte auf den Tafeln, die sich bei symmetrisch ausgerichteten Schlangentafeln ebenso zeigt wie bei kunstvoll arrangierten Muscheln oder Insekten. Somit enthalten die Illustrationen wie die Sammlung immer zwei Aspekte: Sie dienen gleichzeitig der wissenschaftlichen Belehrung und dem ästhetischen Vergnügen.

Der Thesaurus erschloss ein bedeutendes Naturalienkabinett des frühen 18. Jahrhunderts. Die eigentlich stationäre Sammlung wurde als Buch beweglich und für viele Interessenten dauerhaft verfügbar – auch dann noch, als die Sammlung selbst schon Jahrzehnte in alle Winde zerstreut war.

Der vorliegende Band zeigt eine Auswahl der prächtigsten Schmetterlinge und Insekten des 4. Bandes der Originalausgabe.

9.

11.

16.

La collection d'histoire naturelle d'ALBERTUS SEBA
et son INVENTAIRE ILLUSTRÉ

IRMGARD MÜSCH

En devenant apothicaire, Albertus Seba, né en 1665 à Etzel, dans la partie orientale de la Frise, avait choisi une profession qui était étroitement liée à l'étude de l'histoire naturelle. Les médicaments ne s'obtenaient pas par synthèse, mais à partir de composants naturels. Pour tirer leurs remèdes des règnes animal, végétal et minéral, les connaisseurs disposaient de toute une série de recettes transmises par la tradition. Mais beaucoup cherchaient des manières nouvelles d'opérer, et collectionnaient à cet effet des objets de la nature en provenance des quatre coins du monde, dont ils étudiaient et testaient les usages possibles. Bien souvent, cette passion de collectionneur et de chercheur dépassait son utilité pharmaceutique immédiate. Il n'était pas rare de voir des apothicaires constituer d'importantes collections d'histoire naturelle et contribuer ainsi à une connaissance toujours plus grande de la nature.

Son entreprise, que Seba appela « La pharmacie allemande », lui valut rapidement une bonne réputation. Son habileté en affaires valut à Seba l'énorme succès financier grâce auquel il a pu payer son importante collection d'objets naturels. Evidemment, il ne se contentait pas seulement de la clientèle de passage. Il s'était aussi lancé dans le commerce des matières premières pharmaceutiques (drogues) d'outre-mer, dont il faisait la publicité dans une revue d'Amsterdam, en y indiquant les prix. Par ailleurs, il fournissait des pharmacies de voyage aux bateaux en partance et soignait les marins. Certaines sources racontent qu'il se précipitait au port à l'arrivée des bateaux, pour traiter les matelots avec ses remèdes. Il parvenait ainsi à acheter à bon prix à ces hommes épuisés des objets de la nature ou à les échanger contre des médicaments.

En s'installant à Amsterdam, Seba n'aurait guère pu trouver un lieu plus propice à la constitution d'une collection d'histoire naturelle et il réussit à constituer une collection imposante dont la renommée dépassa les frontières d'Amsterdam.

LE THESAURUS D'ALBERTUS SEBA

Le 30 octobre 1731, un contrat tripartite fut conclu à Amsterdam : les représentants de deux éditeurs et Seba convinrent de publier le contenu du cabinet de l'apothicaire dans un grand ouvrage d'environ 400 planches. Effectivement, le Thesaurus arbore 446 planches, dont 175 sous forme de double page. Les quatre volumes sont parus en l'espace de 30 ans, de 1734 jusqu'en 1765. Les explications qui accompagnaient les planches étaient chaque fois publiées en deux versions : l'une latino-française, l'autre latino-néerlandaise. En effet, Seba s'adressait avec son Thesaurus à un public international de naturalistes, de collectionneurs et de bibliophiles. Le texte des deux premiers volumes fut, dans une grande mesure, écrit par Seba lui-même, mais il se fit aider par d'autres naturalistes. Les quelques pages au début du premier volume du Thesaurus présentent des reproductions de squelettes de plantes, que Seba avait préparés et conservés à l'aide d'une technique spéciale. Les images suivantes étaient des représentations d'animaux et de plantes d'Amérique du Sud et d'Asie. Outre des lézards, des oiseaux, des grenouilles, des araignées et d'autres espèces, il représenta aussi des animaux légendaires, tels que les dragons. Le deuxième volume est avant tout consacré aux serpents, mais quelques plantes et animaux figurent également sur ses planches, à des fins décoratives et pour représenter la façon de vivre des reptiles. Le milieu marin fait l'objet du troisième volume où un nombre impressionnant d'animaux tels que coquillages, étoiles de mer, pieuvres, oursins et poissons attendent le lecteur. Le dernier volume présente sur une centaine de planches une vaste collection d'insectes, suivie sur quelques pages de représentations des minéraux et fossiles du cabinet de Seba.

La publication d'une œuvre telle que le Thesaurus nécessita d'importants moyens financiers. Surtout, les nombreuses planches, dont la réalisation demanda beaucoup de temps, générèrent des coûts immenses. Ainsi connaît-on les noms de pas moins de 13 artistes, qui transférèrent sur plaques les planches, le frontispice et le portrait. Cet ouvrage luxueux parut d'abord en noir et blanc. Nous ignorons si les éditeurs eux-mêmes ont proposé une version colorée, ce qui aurait évidemment considérablement augmenté le prix et la marge bénéficiaire. Il est probable que les acheteurs faisaient colorier leur livre à leurs propres frais, et qu'ils s'adressaient à cet effet à des coloristes spécialisés. La beauté des couleurs offre un plaisir particulier. Mais outre l'attrait esthétique, ce coloriage revêtait aussi une utilité scientifique. Par exemple, certains spécimens de papillons, de serpents ou de coquillages ne se distinguent que par leurs couleurs, et les différences de motifs ne sont guère visibles en noir et blanc.

Avec ou sans couleur, reprenant des images existantes ou non, le Thesaurus est en tout cas un exemple impressionnant et convaincant de l'art baroque du livre. Les planches des volumes deux à quatre correspondent de plus en plus à une présentation scientifique caractéristique de l'époque. Les animaux sont présentés les uns après les autres – soigneusement séparés par genre. Pour rendre les illustrations aussi lisibles que possible, les animaux ne se recouvrent jamais et leurs grandeurs respectives sont respectées. Il reste le principe de l'arrangement ornemental des objets sur les planches, que l'on observe aussi bien sur les illustrations de serpents à structure symétrique qu'avec les coquillages ou les insectes disposés avec art. Ainsi, les illustrations et les collections présentent toujours un double intérêt : l'instruction scientifique et le plaisir esthétique.

Le Thesaurus a fait découvrir au public un important cabinet d'histoire naturelle du début du XVIIIe siècle. Grâce au livre, la collection qui était stationnaire à l'origine, est devenue mobile et accessible à un large public d'intéressés, pendant encore des décennies après avoir été dispersée à tous vents.

Cette publication présente un choix représentatif d'illustrations de papillons et d'insectes du quatrième volume de l'édition originale.

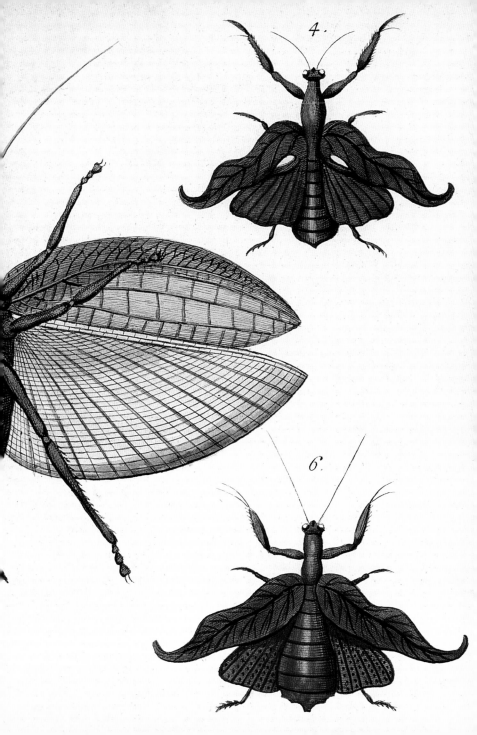

La colección de Historia Natural de ALBERTUS SEBA y su INVENTARIO GRÁFICO

IRMGARD MÜSCH

Albertus Seba, nacido en Etzel (Frisia oriental) en 1665, eligió la profesión de boticario, un oficio en aquel entonces estrechamente relacionado con los estudios de Historia Natural. En aquel tiempo, los medicamentos no se fabricaban sintéticamente como hoy en día, sino que se obtenían mezclando elementos naturales. Para conseguir las sustancias curativas de animales, plantas y minerales se disponía de toda una serie de recetas tradicionales. Sin embargo, muchos buscaban nuevas vías, coleccionaban objetos naturales de los cuatro puntos cardinales y estudiaban y ensayaban su posible aplicación. En muchos casos la pasión coleccionista e investigadora se emancipó del uso meramente farmacéutico; numerosos boticarios crearon colecciones de Historia Natural de consideración, contribuyendo así a un mejor conocimiento de la Naturaleza.

Con su comercio, que denominaba «La farmacopea alemana», Seba se granjeó pronto un gran prestigio. Al gran éxito de su botica, lo cual le permitió crear su extensa colección, contribuyó el hecho de que Seba fue un buen comerciante y no confió únicamente en clientes ocasionales; antes al contrario negoció con materias primas farmacéuticas (drogas) de fuera de Europa, para las que hacía publicidad –indicando el precio– en un periódico de Ámsterdam. Se ocupaba asimismo de la botica de viaje de los barcos que soltaban amarras en el puerto de dicha ciudad, así como de tratar a los marineros. Según la tradición, cuando un barco anclaba en el puerto, Seba se apresuraba a tratar a los marineros y conseguía comprar a buen precio los objetos que traían de lejanos países, o los obtenía por trueque con medicamentos.

Seba no pudo encontrar mejor lugar que Ámsterdam como base para crear una colección de Historia Natural; así reunió una colección cuyo prestigio llegaba hasta muy lejos de las fronteras de Ámsterdam.

EL THESAURUS DE ALBERTUS SEBA

El 30 de octubre de 1731 se cerró en Ámsterdam un acuerdo entre tres partes: los representantes de dos editoriales y Seba se pusieron de acuerdo para publicar el gabinete del coleccionista en una gran obra, acompañada de unos 400 cuadros. En realidad, el Thesaurus contiene nada menos que 446 tablas, 175 de ellas a doble plana. Los cuatro volúmenes de la obra se publicaron a lo largo de 30 años: de 1734 a 1765. Los textos explicativos de las ilustraciones aparecieron en dos versiones bilingües: en latín-francés y latín-neerlandés, pues Seba quería dirigirse con el Thesaurus a un público internacional de investigadores de la naturaleza, coleccionistas y amantes de los libros. Gran parte del texto del primer volumen lo escribió Seba mismo, si bien contó con la ayuda de otros investigadores. Al principio del primer volumen se encuentran unas páginas con ilustraciones de esqueletos de plantas, que Seba trató y conservó con una técnica especial. A continuación, el Thesaurus presenta representaciones de fauna y flora suramericana y asiática: junto a lagartos, pájaros, sapos, arañas y otros animales aparecen animales de fábula como dragones. El volumen II está dedicado principalmente a las serpientes; sin embargo, con fines decorativos y para ilustrar el modo de vida de los reptiles, se pueden ver algunas plantas y otros animales en las ilustraciones. El volumen III trata el ámbito vital acuático: el observador puede apreciar una gran variedad de animales del mar: moluscos, estrellas de mar, pulpos, erizos de mar y peces. El último volumen presenta, en casi 100 tablas, una nutrida colección de insectos, seguida de algunas páginas con representaciones de minerales y fósiles procedentes del gabinete de Seba.

La empresa de editar una obra como el Thesaurus exigió un amplio despliegue de medios económicos. Sobre todo las numerosas ilustraciones, cuya elaboración exigía mucho tiempo, causaron enormes gastos. Se conoce con su nombre a 13 artistas, que se ocuparon únicamente de trasladar a planchas las tablas, el frontispicio y el retrato. La costosa obra se publicó inicialmente en blanco y negro. No se sabe si las editoriales habían ofrecido también una edición coloreada, que naturalmente habría aumentado considerablemente el precio y el margen de beneficios. Es de suponer que los compradores la encargaran a especialistas en el coloreado, corriendo ellos con los gastos. La riqueza de color es un verdadero placer; pero el coloreado no solo elevaba el atractivo estético, sino también el valor científico. Por ejemplo, algunos ejemplares de mariposas, serpientes o moluscos solo se distinguen con la ayuda del color, mientras que en blanco y negro es muy difícil reconocer las diferencias entre algunos animales. Con o sin coloración, el Thesaurus es en cualquier caso un ejemplo impresionante del arte barroco de la imprenta. Las tablas de los volúmenes segundo a cuarto responden cada vez más a la presentación científica usual en aquella época. Los animales se presentan cuidadosamente clasificados por géneros. Para que las ilustraciones resulten lo más legibles posible se reproducen los animales sin interferencias y en una escala única; ahora bien, con los lados invertidos, lo cual -en el caso de los caracoles con la casa girada a la izquierda- produjo ciertos malentendidos. Se ha conservado la distribución ornamental de los objetos en las ilustraciones, como se aprecia tanto en la simetría de las tablas de serpientes como en la artística distribución de moluscos o insectos. De este modo, tanto las ilustraciones como la colección adquiere siempre un doble aspecto: sirven tanto para la formación científica como para el placer estético.

El Thesaurus divulgó un importante gabinete de Historia Natural de comienzos del siglo XVIII. La colección, en realidad fija, adquirió movilidad gracias a su publicación: muchas personas interesadas pudieron recurrir a ella, incluso cuando hacía ya decenios que la colección se había dispersado en todas las direcciones.

El presente volumen muestra una selección de las magníficos mariposas y de los insectos del cuarto volumen de la edición original.

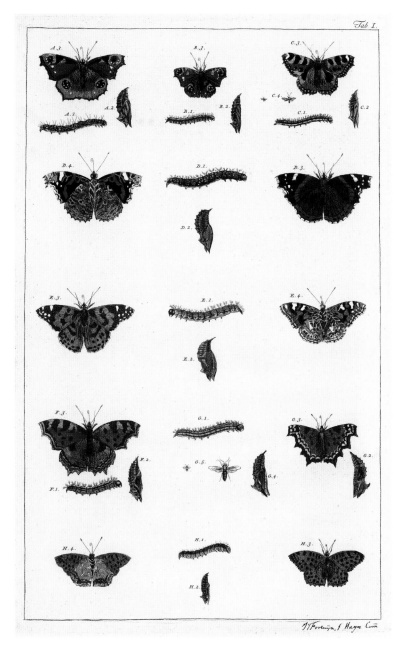

Tab I.

A–B Peacocks · Tagpfauenaugen · Paons de jour · Pavo real **C1–3** Small tortoiseshell · Kleiner Fuchs · Petite tortue ·
Ortiguera **D** Red admiral · Admiral · Vulcain · Vanesa **C4, G5** Wasps and bees · Hautflügler · Hyménoptères ·
Himenópteros **E** Painted lady · Distelfalter · Belle-dame · Cardera **F** Large tortoiseshell · Großer Fuchs · Grande tortue ·
Mariposa de los olmos **G1–4** Comma butterfly · C-Falter · Robert-le-diable · Mariposa de la coma

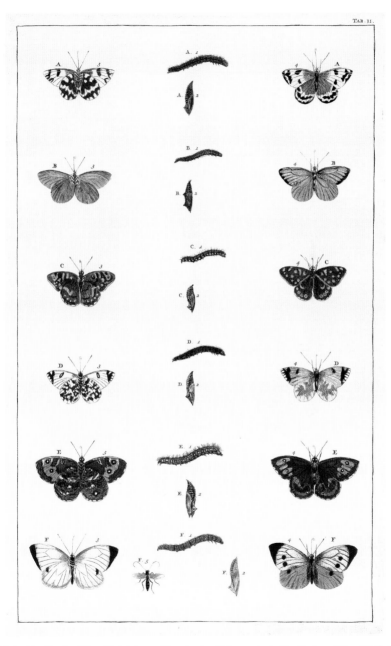

A Bath white · Resedaweißling · Marbré de vert · Blanquiverdosa **B** Green-veined white · Heckenweißling · Piéride du navet · Oruga de las coles **C3-4** Specled wood · Laubfalter · Tircis · Mariposa de los muros **D3-4** Orange tip · Aurorafalter · Aurore printanière · Aurora verdirrayada **E3-4** Rock grayling · Rostbinde · Agreste · Sátiro común **F1-4** Large white · Großer Kohlweißling · Piéride du chou · Blanca de la col **F5** Ichneumon wasp · Schlupfwespe · Ichneumon · Icneumón

Tab XLIII

Tropical butterflies and moths from
America · Tropische Tag- und
Nachtfalter aus Amerika · Papillons
diurnes et nocturnes tropicaux
d'Amérique · Mariposas diurnas y
nocturnas de la América tropical

TAB. III.

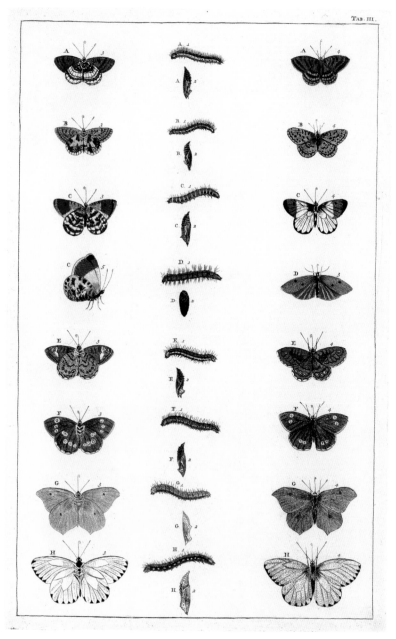

A Scarce fritillary · Eschenscheckenfalter · Damier du frêne · Euphydryas **C3–5** Orange tip · Aurorafalter · Aurore printanière · Aurora verdirrayada **D** Large footman · Mittelwald-Flechtenbär · Lithosie quadrille · Oruga fitófaga de líquenes **E3–4** Brown · Augenfalter · Satyridé · Satyridae **F3–4** Arran brown · Milchfleck · Grand nègre hongrois · Erebia **G3–4** Common brimstone · Zitronenfalter · Citron · Mariposa limonera **H** Black-veined white · Baumweißling · Gazé · Blanca del majuelo

Tab. IV

Butterflies from tropical America · Tagfalter aus dem tropischen Amerika · Papillons diurnes d'Amérique tropicale ·
Mariposas diurnas de la América tropical

Tropical butterflies distributed worldwide and caddis flies · Tropische Tagfalter mit weltweiter Verbreitung und Köcherfliegen · Papillons diurnes tropicaux répandus dans le monde entier et trichoptères · Mariposas tropicales diurnas con difusión mundial y Trichoptera

Tab. V.

Butterflies from America, Africa, Arabia and the region encompassing South-East Asia to North Australia ·
Tagfalter aus Amerika, Afrika, Arabien und von Südostasien bis nach Nordaustralien ·
Papillons diurnes d'Amérique, d'Afrique, d'Arabie et de la zone Asie du Sud-Est – Australie du Nord ·
Mariposas de América, África, Arabia y desde el sureste asiático hasta el norte de Australia

Butterflies from South America and South-East Asia · Tagfalter aus Südamerika und Südostasien ·
Papillons diurnes d'Amérique du Sud et d'Asie du Sud-Est · Mariposas de América del Sur y del sureste asiático

Tab. VIII.

Butterflies distributed variously from South America, the region encompassing the Malay Archipelago to Australia, and worldwide · Tagfalter aus Südamerika, vom Malaiischen Archipel bis nach Australien und mit weltweiter Verbreitung · Papillons diurnes originaires d'Amérique du Sud, de la zone de l'Archipel indomalais – Australie, et répandus dans le monde entier · Mariposas diurnas de América del Sur, desde el Archipiélago Malayo hasta Australia y otras con difusión mundial

Tab. IX.

Butterflies from the Malay Archipelago and New Guinea · Tagfalter aus dem Malaiischen Archipel und Neuguinea · Papillons diurnes de l'Archipel indomalais et de Nouvelle-Guinée · Mariposas del Archipiélago Malayo y Nueva Guinea

Butterflies from tropical America · Tagfalter aus dem tropischen Amerika ·
Papillons diurnes d'Amérique tropicale · Mariposas diurnas de la América tropical

Tab. XLIV.

Butterflies from tropical
America and the region
encompassing South-East
Asia to Australia · Tag-
falter aus dem tropischen
Amerika und von Süd-
ostasien bis nach Austra-
lien · Papillons diurnes
d'Amérique tropicale
et de la zone Asie du
Sud-Est – Australie ·
Mariposas diurnas de la
América tropical y desde
el sureste asiático hasta
Australia

Tab. XI.

Butterflies from South America and the region encompassing the Malay Archipelago and New Guinea to Australia ·
Tagfalter aus Südamerika und vom Malaiischen Archipel und Neuguinea bis nach Australien ·
Papillons diurnes d'Amérique du Sud et de la zone de l'Archipel indomalais et de Nouvelle-Guinée – Australie ·
Mariposas diurnas de América del Sur y desde el Archipiélago Malayo y Nueva Guinea hasta Australia

Butterflies and hawkmoths from Europe and tropical Central and South America · Tagfalter und Schwärmer aus Europa
und dem tropischen Mittel- und Südamerika · Papillons diurnes et sphinx d'Europe et des zones tropicales
d'Amérique Centrale et du Sud · Mariposas y sphingidae de Europa y de la América tropical Central y del Sur

38

Tab. XIII.

Butterflies from the tropics of America and the Caribbean · Tagfalter aus den Tropen Amerikas und der Karibik ·
Papillons diurnes des zones tropicales d'Amérique et des Caraïbes · Mariposas diurnas de las zonas tropicales
de América y del Caribe

Tropical butterflies distributed worldwide · Tropische Tagfalter mit weltweiter Verbreitung ·
Papillons diurnes tropicaux répandus dans le monde entier · Mariposas diurnas tropicales con difusión mundial

40

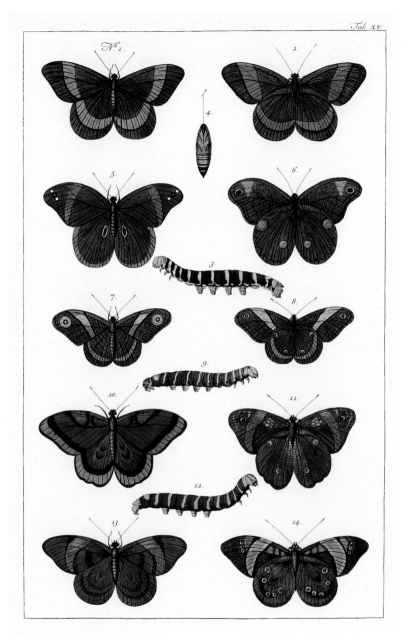

Butterflies from tropical Central and South America and the Indo-Australian faunal region ·
Tagfalter aus dem tropischen Mittel- und Südamerika und dem indo-australischen Faunengebiet ·
Papillons diurnes des zones tropicales d'Amérique Centrale et du Sud, et de la région faunique indo-australienne ·
Mariposas diurnas de las zonas tropicales de América Central y del Sur y de la región de la fauna indo-australiana

Butterflies from the Malay Archipelago and New Guinea to Australia · Tagfalter vom Malaiischen Archipel
und Neuguinea bis nach Australien · Papillons diurnes de la zone de l'Archipel indomalais et de
Nouvelle-Guinée–Australie · Mariposas diurnas de la zona del Archipiélago Malayo y de Nueva-Guinea hasta Australia

42

Butterflies from tropical Central and South America · Tagfalter aus dem tropischen Mittel- und Südamerika ·
Papillons diurnes des zones tropicales d'Amérique Centrale et du Sud · Mariposas diurnas de las zonas tropicales
de América Central y del Sur

Tab. XVIII

Butterflies distributed worldwide · Tagfalter mit weltweiter Verbreitung ·
Papillons diurnes répandus dans le monde entier · Mariposas diurnas de difusión mundial

Butterflies from South-East Asia, North Australia and Central and South America · Tagfalter aus Südostasien, Nordaustralien und Mittel- und Südamerika · Papillons diurnes d'Asie du Sud-Est, d'Australie du Nord et d'Amérique Centrale et du Sud · Mariposas diurnas del sureste asiático, del norte de Australia y de América Central y del Sur

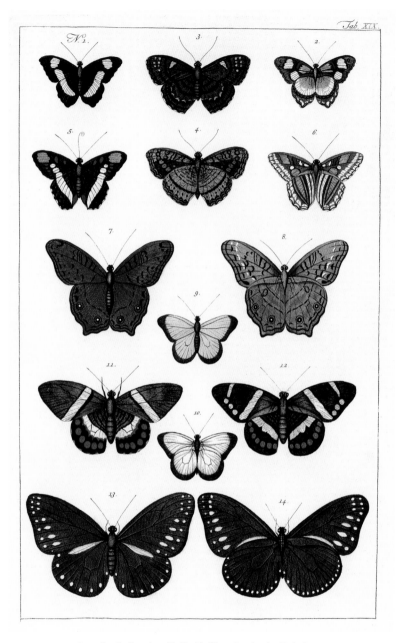

Butterflies distributed worldwide · Tagfalter mit weltweiter Verbreitung ·
Papillons diurnes répandus dans le monde entier · Mariposas diurnas con difusión mundial

Butterflies from tropical South America · Tagfalter aus dem tropischen Südamerika ·
Papillons diurnes des zones tropicales d'Amérique du Sud · Mariposas diurnas de la América del Sur tropical

Tab XXI

Butterflies and moths from South America and Eurasia · Tag- und Nachtfalter aus Südamerika und Eurasien ·
Papillons diurnes et nocturnes d'Amérique du Sud et d'Eurasie · Mariposas diurnas y nocturnas de América del Sur y Eurasia

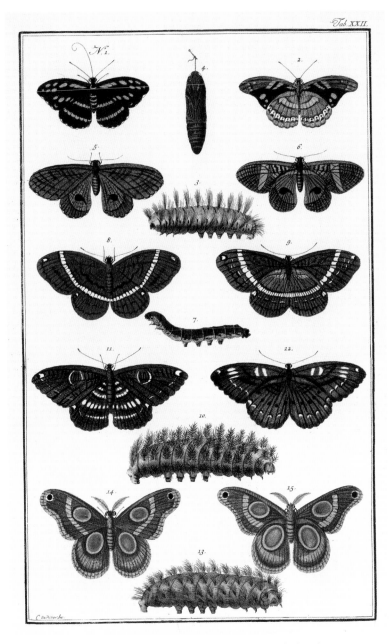

Butterflies from Indonesia and New Guinea and silkmoths from Central and South America ·
Tagfalter aus Indonesien und Neuguinea sowie Augenspinner aus Mittel- und Südamerika ·
Papillons diurnes d'Indonésie et de Nouvelle-Guinée ainsi que saturniidés d'Amérique Centrale et du Sud ·
Mariposas diurnas de Indonesia y de Nueva Guinea, así como Saturniidae de América Central y del Sur

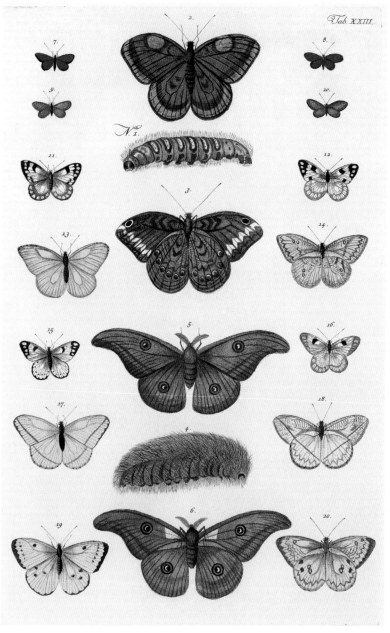

Tab. XXIII.

Butterflies from Europe, America and North Africa and silkmoths from South-East Asia ·
Tagfalter aus Europa, Amerika und Nordafrika sowie Augenspinner aus Südostasien ·
Papillons diurnes d'Europe, d'Amérique et d'Afrique du Nord ainsi que saturniidés d'Asie du Sud-Est ·
Mariposas diurnas de Europa, América y norte de África, así como Saturniidae del sureste asiático

Butterflies and tiger moths from South America · Tagfalter und Bärenspinner aus Südamerika ·
Papillons diurnes et arctiidés d'Amérique du Sud · Mariposas diurnas y Arctiidae de América del Sur

Tab. XXV.

One dragonfly, butterflies and silkmoths from South-East Asia to Australia · Eine Libelle, Tagfalter und Augenspinner von Südostasien bis Australien · Une libellule, des papillons diurnes ainsi que des saturniidés de la zone Asie du Sud-Est–Australie · Una libélula, mariposas diurnas, así como Saturniidae desde el sureste asiático hasta Australia

Butterflies from Africa, Central and South America and the Moluccas · Tagfalter aus Afrika, Mittel- und Südamerika und den Molukken · Papillons diurnes d'Afrique, d'Amérique Centrale et du Sud et des Moluques · Mariposas de África, América Central y del Sur y de las Molucas

Tab. XLVI.

Butterflies from
South-East Asia and
North Africa · Tag-
falter aus Südostasien
und Nordafrika ·
Papillons diurnes
d'Asie du Sud-Est et
d'Afrique du Nord ·
Mariposas diurnas
del sureste asiático y
del norte de África

Butterflies and moths from South America and South-East Asia · Tag- und Nachtfalter aus
Südamerika und Südostasien · Papillons diurnes et nocturnes d'Amérique du Sud et d'Asie du Sud-Est ·
Mariposas diurnas y nocturnas de América del Sur y del sureste asiático

Tab. XXVIII.

Tropical butterflies distributed worldwide · Tropische Tagfalter mit weltweiter Verbreitung ·
Papillons diurnes tropicaux répandus dans le monde entier · Mariposas diurnas tropicales con difusión mundial

Tab. XXIX.

Butterflies from Africa and tropical Central and South America · Tagfalter aus Afrika und dem tropischen Mittel- und Südamerika · Papillons diurnes d'Afrique et des zones tropicales d'Amérique Centrale et du Sud · Mariposas diurnas de África y de las zonas tropicales de América Central y del Sur

Tab. XXX.

Butterflies from tropical America and the region encompassing Africa to Arabia · Tagfalter aus dem tropischen Amerika und von Afrika bis nach Arabien · Papillons diurnes d'Amérique tropicale et de la zone d'Afrique–Arabie · Mariposas diurnas de la América tropical y desde África hasta Arabia

Tab. XXXII.

1–2, 5–6 Camberwell beauties · Trauermäntel · Morios · Nymphalis antiopa **3–4** Peacock · Tagpfauenauge ·
Paon-de-jour · Pavo real **7–10** (Common yellow) swallowtail/Old World swallowtail · Schwalbenschwanz ·
Grand porte-queue · Mariposa macaón **11–12** Scarce swallowtail · Segelfalter · Flambé · Podalirio

Tab. XXXI

Butterflies from tropical Central and South America · Tagfalter aus dem tropischen Mittel- und Südamerika ·
Papillons diurnes des zones tropicales d'Amérique Centrale et du Sud · Mariposas diurnas de las zonas
tropicales de América Central y del Sur

Tab. XXXIII.

Butterflies from tropical Central and South America · Tagfalter aus dem tropischen Mittel- und Südamerika ·
Papillons diurnes des zones tropicales d'Amérique Centrale et du Sud · Mariposas diurnas de las zonas
tropicales de América Central y del Sur

Butterflies from America and South-East Asia · Tagfalter aus Amerika und Südostasien ·
Papillons diurnes d'Amérique et d'Asie du Sud-Est · Mariposas diurnas de América y del sureste asiático

Butterflies from the
Malay Archipelago,
New Guinea and
Australia · Tagfalter
aus dem Malaiischen
Archipel, Neuguinea
und Australien ·
Papillons diurnes
de l'Archipel indo-
malais, de Nouvelle-
Guinée et d'Australie ·
Mariposas diurnas del
Archipiélago Malayo,
Nueva Guinea y
Australia

Tab. XXXV.

Butterflies from Africa, tropical America, from South-East Asia to Australia, as well as one South American moth ·
Tagfalter aus Afrika, dem tropischen Amerika, von Südostasien bis nach Australien sowie ein südamerikanischer Nachtfalter ·
Papillons diurnes d'Afrique et d'Amérique tropicale, d'Asie du Sud-Est – Australie, ainsi qu'un papillon nocturne d'Amérique
du Sud · Mariposas diurnas de África, de la América tropical y desde el sureste asiático hasta Australia

Tab. XXXVI

Butterflies distributed variously in tropical and subtropical America and worldwide · Tagfalter aus dem tropischen und subtropischen Amerika und mit weltweiter Verbreitung · Papillons originaires d'Amérique tropicale et subtropicale, et répandus dans le monde entier · Mariposas diurnas de la América tropical y subtropical y con difusión mundial

Tab. XXXVII.

Butterflies distributed variously from South-East Asia to Australia, and worldwide · Tagfalter von Südostasien bis nach
Australien und mit weltweiter Verbreitung · Papillons diurnes originaires de la zone d'Asie du Sud-Est–Australie,
et répandus dans le monde entier · Mariposas diurnas desde el sureste asiático hasta Australia y con difusión mundial

Tab. XXXVIII.

Butterflies from tropical and subtropical America · Tagfalter aus dem tropischen und subtropischen Amerika ·
Papillons diurnes d'Amérique tropicale et subtropicale · Mariposas diurnas de la América tropical y subtropical

Tab. XXXIX.

Butterflies from South America and Africa and moths from Malay Archipelago, New Guinea and America · Tagfalter aus
Südamerika und Afrika sowie Nachtfalter aus dem Malaiischen Archipel, Neuguinea und Amerika · Papillons diurnes
d'Amérique du Sud et d'Afrique, et papillons nocturnes de l'Archipel indomalais, de Nouvelle-Guinée ainsi que d'Amérique ·
Mariposas diurnas de América del Sur y de África, así como nocturnas del Archipiélago Malayo, Nueva Guinea y América

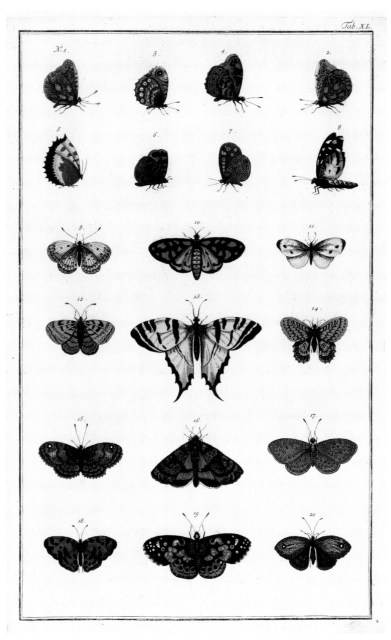

Butterflies and moths from Eurasia and America · Schmetterlinge aus Eurasien und Amerika ·
Papillons et teignes d'Eurasie et d'Amérique · Lepidópteros de Eurasia y América

Tropical butterflies distributed worldwide · Tropische Tagfalter mit weltweiter Verbreitung ·
Papillons diurnes tropicaux répandus dans le monde entier · Mariposas diurnas tropicales con difusión mundial

Butterflies and moths from Central and South America and the region encompassing tropical Africa to Australia ·
Tag- und Nachtfalter aus Mittel- und Südamerika und vom tropischen Afrika bis nach Australien ·
Papillons diurnes et nocturnes d'Amérique Centrale et du Sud et de la zone d'Afrique tropicale – Australie ·
Mariposas diurnas y nocturnas de América Central y del Sur y desde la África tropical hasta Australia

Tab.LVII.

Very large tropical moths from
South-East Asia and tropical
America · Sehr große tropische
Nachtfalter aus Südostasien
und dem tropischen Amerika ·
Très grands papillons nocturnes
d'Asie du Sud-Est et d'Amérique
tropicale · Muy grandes mariposas
nocturnas tropicales del sureste
asiático y de la América tropical

Tab. XLVIII

D Large yellow underwing · Hausmutter · Fiancée · Noctua pronuba **F1**, **F3**, **F6** Buff-tip · Mondvogel/Ochsenkopf ·
Lunule · Falera **H7** Mottled umber · Großer Frostspanner · Hibernie défeuillante · Erannis defoliaria **I8** Pale prominent ·
Palpen-Zahnspinner · Museau · Pterostoma palpinum **K9** Leopard moth · Kastanienbohrer · Zeuzère du poirier ·
Taladro de la madera **L10** Clouded buff · Rotrandbär · Bordure ensanglantée · Diacrisia sannio

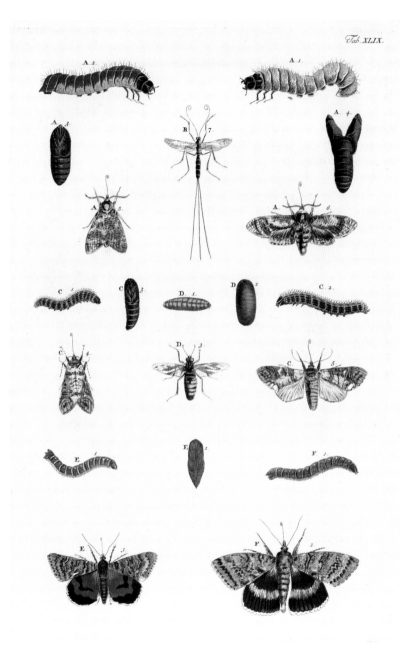

Tab. XLIX.

A1–6 Goat moth · Weidenbohrer · Cossus gâte-bois · Taladro rojo **B7** Ichneumon wasp · Schlupf- und Brackwespe ·
Ichneumon · Icneumón y Minadora de hojas **C1–5** Buff-tip · Mondvogel/Ochsenkopf · Lunule · Falera **D1–2** Diptera · Zwei-
flügler · Diptère · Dípteros **D3** Cimbicid · Knopfhorn-Blattwespe · Cimbicidé · Cimbex lutea **E1–3** Underwing · Ordensband ·
Likenée · Catocala nupcial **F1–2** Clifden nonpareil · Blaues Ordensband · Likenée bleue · Noctuido de los fresnos

Tab. L.

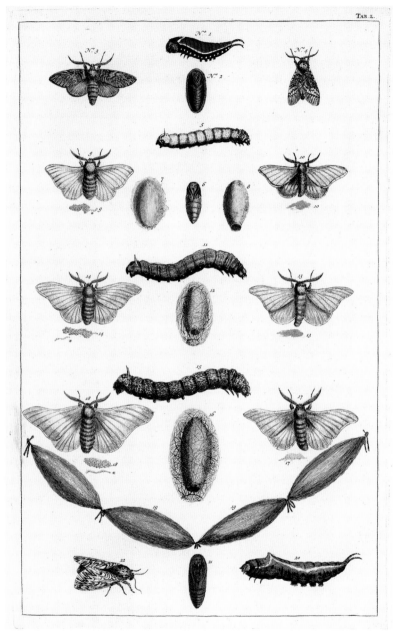

1–4, 20–22 Puss moths · Große Gabelschwänze · Queues fourchues · Grandes fúrculas **5–18** Silkworm-moths ·
Maulbeer-Seidenspinner · Bombyx du mûrier · Gusano de la seda

Tab. LI.

B Fox moth · Brombeerspinner · Anneau du diable · Macrothylacia rubi **C** Clouded buff · Rotrandbär · Bordure ensanglantée ·
Diacrisia sannio **D** Oak eggar · Großer Eichenspinner · Minime à bandes jaunes · Lasiocampa quercus
K Oak hawkmoth · Eichenschwärmer · Sphinx du chêne · Esfinge del roble **L** Four-spotted footman · *Lithosia quadra* ·
Lithosie quadrillé · Oruga fitófaga de líquenes **M** Goat moth · Weidenbohrer · Cossus gâte-bois · Taladro rojo

TAB. LII.

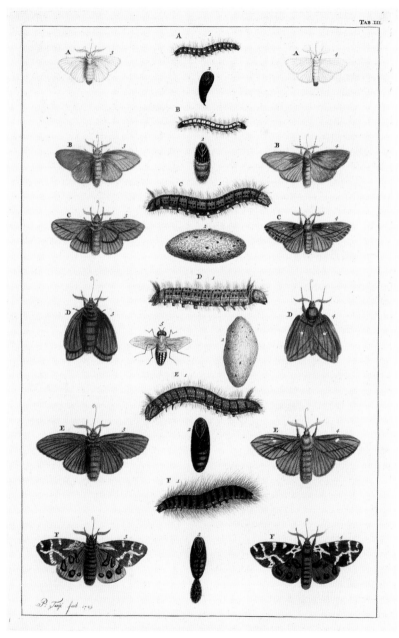

A Yellow-tail · Schwan · Cul-doré · Euproctis similis **B** White satin moth · Pappelspinner · Papillon satiné ·
Mariposa blanca del sauce **C** Drinker · Grasglucke · Buveuse · Philudoria potatoria **D1–4** Oak eggar ·
Großer Eichenspinner · Minime à bandes jaunes · Lasiocampa quercus **D5** Fly · Fliege · Mouche · Mosca
F Garden tiger/Woolly bear · Brauner Bär · Ecaille martre · Arctia caja

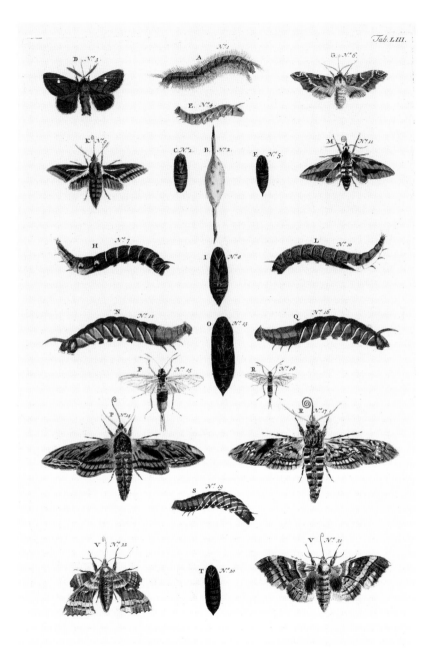

Tab. LIII.

A1–D3 Drinker · Grasglucke · Buveuse · Philudoria potatoria **H7–K9** Elephant hawkmoth · Mittlerer Weinschwärmer ·
Moyen sphinx de la vigne · Esfinge de la vid **L10, M11** Spurge hawkmoth · Wolfsmilchschwärmer · Sphinx de l'euphorbe ·
Esfinge de las tabaibas **N12–P14** Privet hawkmoth · Ligusterschwärmer · Sphinx du troène · Esfinge del aligustre
Q16–R17 Morning glory sphinx moth · Windenschwärmer · Sphinx du liseron · Esfinge de la correhuela

Tab. LIV.

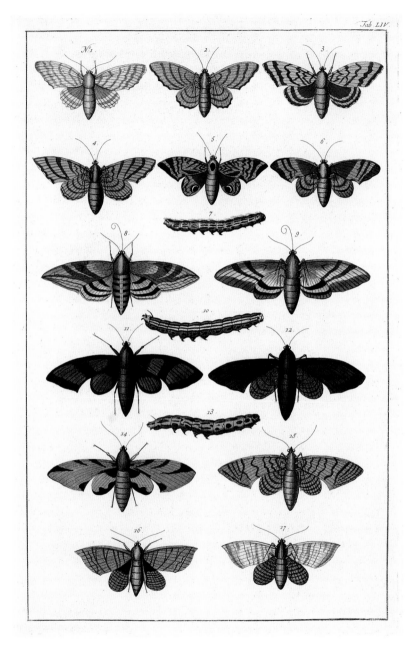

1–2 December eggar · Kleine Pappelglucke · Bombyx du peuplier · Poecilocampa 5–6 Eyed hawkmoth · Abendpfauenauge ·
Sphinx demi-paon · Esfinge ocelada 7 Buff-tip caterpillar · Ochsenkopf-Raupe · Bucéphale/Lunule · Oruga de falera
8–9 Privet hawkmoth · Ligusterschwärmer · Sphinx du troène · Esfinge del aligustre 10–12, 16–17 Hawkmoths · Schwärmer ·
Sphinx · Esfinges 13–15 Mediterranean hawkmoth · Großer Wolfsmilchschwärmer · Sphinx nicéa · Esfinge de las tabaibas

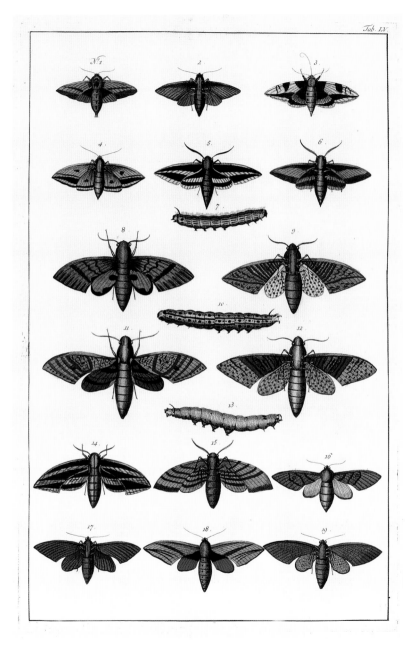

1–19 Hawkmoths · Schwärmer · Sphinx · Esfinges **1–2** Elephant hawkmoths · Mittlere Weinschwärmer ·
Moyen Sphinx de la vigne · Esfinge de la vid **3–4** Spurge hawkmoths · Wolfsmilchschwärmer ·
Sphinx de l'euphorbe · Esfinge de las tabaibas **7** Buff-tip moth · Mondvogel · Phalère bucéphale/Lunule · Falera
11–12 Gaudy sphinx moths · Schwärmer · Sphingidés · Esfinges

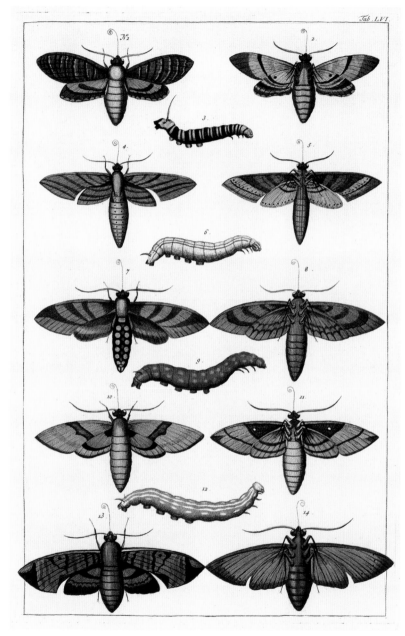

1–14 Hawkmoths · Schwärmer · Sphinx · Esfinges **1–2** Death's head hawkmoth · Totenkopfschwärmer ·
Sphinx tête-de-mort · Esfinge de la calavera **7–8** Occult sphinx · Schwärmer · Sphinx · Esfinge
10–11 Gaudy sphinx moth · Schwärmer · Sphingidé · Esfinge **13–14** Fig sphinx · Schwärmer · Sphingidé · Esfinge

4–6 Eyed hawkmoths · Abendpfauenaugen · Sphinx demi-paon · Esfinge ocelada **12–13** Swallowtails · Schwalbenschwänze ·
Grands porte-queues · Mariposas macaón **14–15** Orange tips · Aurorafalter · Aurores · Auroras verdirrayadas
16–17 Bath whites · Resedaweißlinge · Marbrés de vert · Blanquiverdosas **18** Large emperor · Großes Nachtpfauenauge ·
Grand paon-de-nuit · Pavón nocturno **26–27** Peacocks · Tagpfauenaugen · Automéris · Pavos reales

Very large tropical moths ·
Sehr große tropische Nachtfalter ·
Très grands papillons nocturnes
tropicaux · Mariposas nocturnas
tropicales de muy gran tamaño

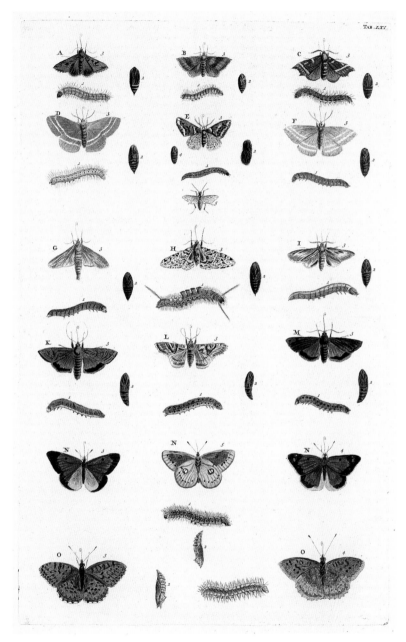

TAB. LXI.

Butterflies and moths from Central Europe with caterpillars and pupae · Tag- und Nachtfalter aus Mitteleuropa
mit Puppen und Raupen · Papillons diurnes et nocturnes d'Europe centrale ainsi que chrysalides et chenilles ·
Mariposas diurnas y nocturnas de Europa Central con crisálidas y orugas

Tab. LXII

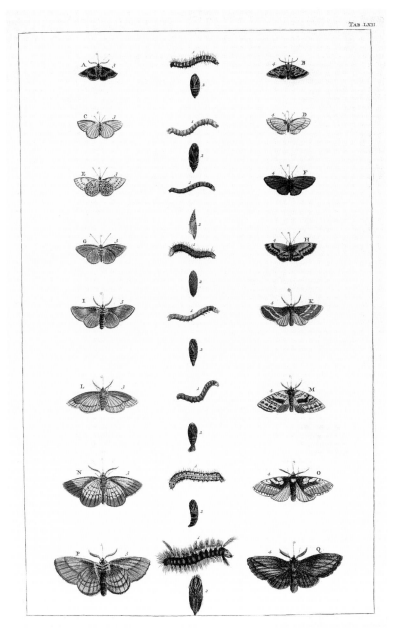

E–F Blues butterflies · Bläulinge · Azurés · Licénidos
P–Q1-4 Dark tussocks · Graue Kleespinner · Pattes étendues agathes · Dicallomera fascelina

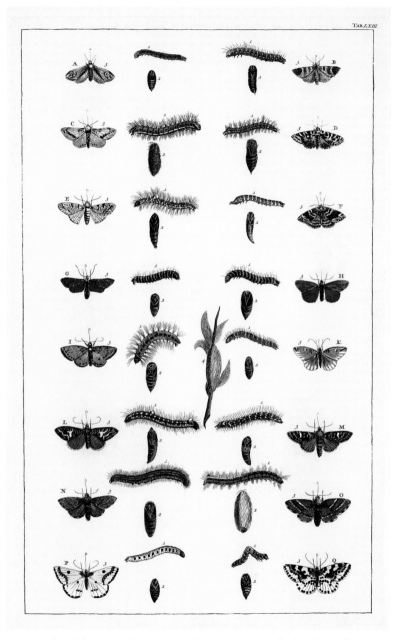

Tab. *LXIII*

G1, H1–3 Cinnabar · Blutbär · Goutte-de-sang · Tyria jacobaeae **G2–3** Burnet · Widderchen/Blutströpfchen · Zygène · Zygaenidae **N1–3** Lackey · Ringelspinner· Livrée des arbres · Lagarta rayada **O1–3** Small eggar · Wollafter/Glucke · Bombyx laineux · Eriogaster lanestris **P3, Q1–3** Currant moth · Stachelbeerspanner · Zérène du groseillier · Abraxas grossulariata

Tab. LXIV.

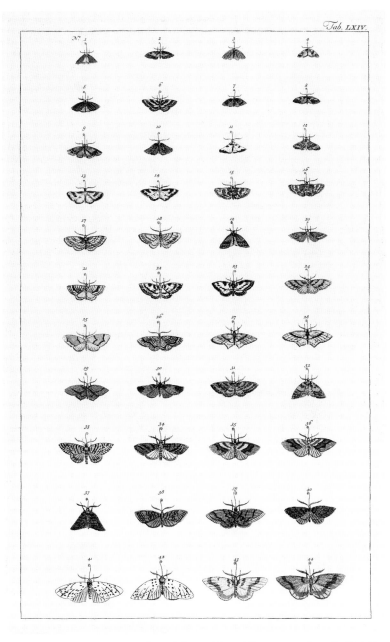

Moths from Central Europe and North Africa, including pyralids, tortricids, geometers and noctuids · Nachtfalter
aus Mitteleuropa und Nordafrika, darunter Zünsler, Wickler, Spanner und Eulenfalter · Papillons de nuit d'Europe
Centrale et d'Afrique du Nord incluant des pyrales, des tordeuses, des géomètres et des noctuelles · Mariposas nocturnas
de Europa Central y del norte de África, incluyendo Pyralidae, Tortricidae, Geometridae y Noctuidae

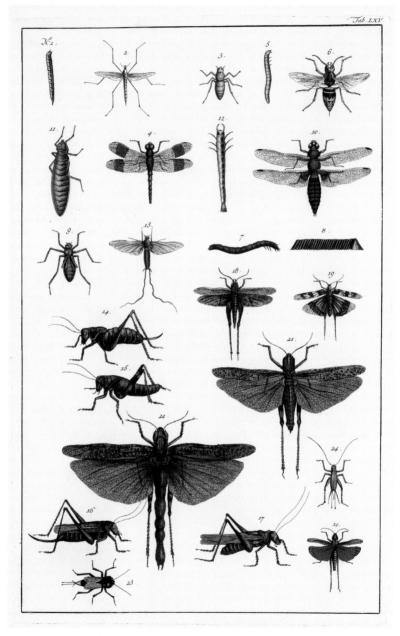

Various insects and insect larvae, chiefly grasshoppers · Verschiedene Insekten und Insektenlarven,
vorwiegend Heuschrecken · Divers insectes et larves d'insectes, principalement des sauterelles ·
Diversos insectos y larvas de insectos, principalmente langostas

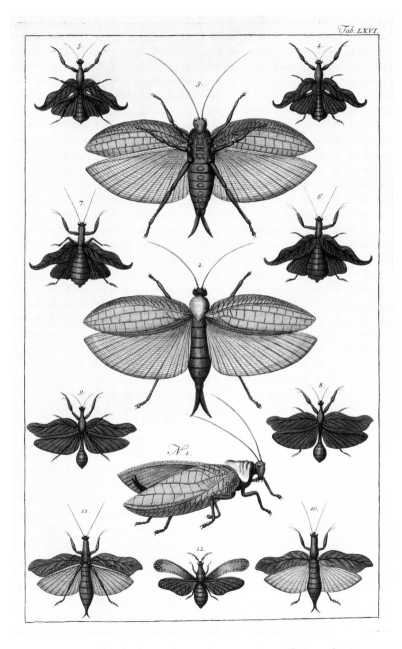

Tab. LXVI.

1–3 Katydids · Langfühlerschrecken · Ensifères · Ensíferas 4–11 Praying mantids · Gottesanbeterinnen ·
Mantes · Mantis religiosas 12 Cicada · Zikade · Hémiptère · Cigarra

Tab. LXVII.

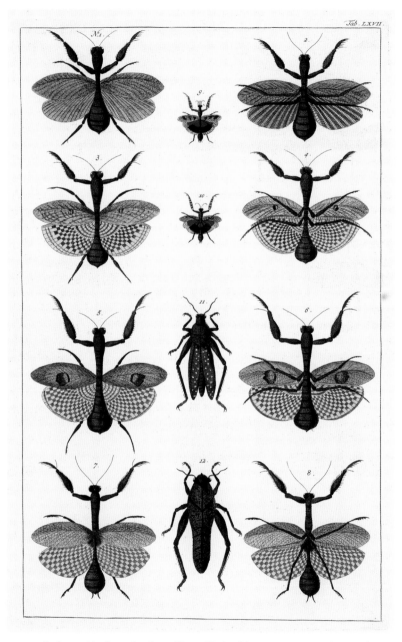

1–10 Praying mantids · Gottesanbeterinnen · Mantes · Mantis religiosas **9–10** European praying mantids ·
Gottesanbeterinnen · Mantes religieuses · Mantis religiosas **11–12** Grasshoppers · Heuschrecken · Criquets · Langostas

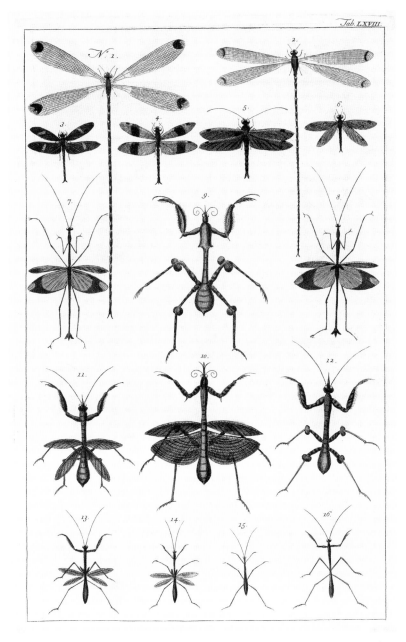

Tab. LXVIII.

1–6 Dragonflies · Libellen · Libellules · Libélulas 7–12 Praying mantids · Gottesanbeterinnen · Mantes · Mantis religiosas
9–12 Gargoyle mantids/Walking violins · Wandelnde Geigen · Violons ambulants · Gongylus gongylodes

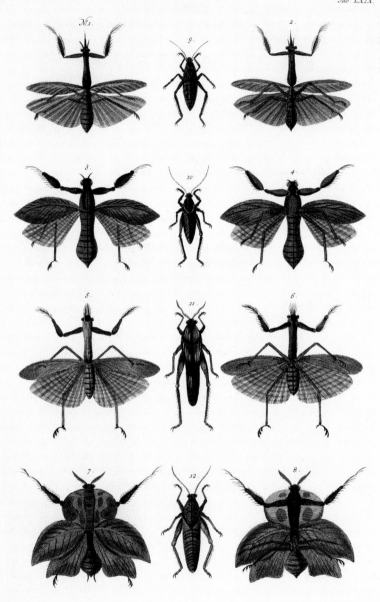

Tab. LXIX.

1–8 Praying mantids · Gottesanbeterinnen · Mantes· Mantis religiosas
9–12 Grasshoppers · Heuschrecken · Orthoptères · Langostas

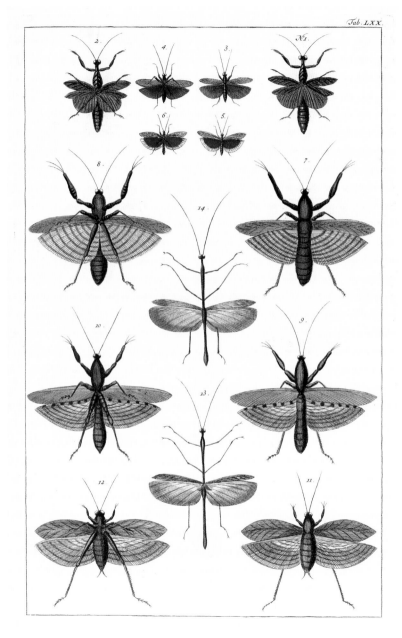

Tab. LXX.

1–2, 7–10, 14–15 Praying mantids · Gottesanbeterinnen · Mantes · Mantis religiosas
3–6, 11–12 Katydids and grasshoppers · Heuschrecken · Sauterelles et criquets · Langostas y saltamontes
13–14 Stick insects · Stabheuschrecke · Phasmes · Sipyloidea sipylus

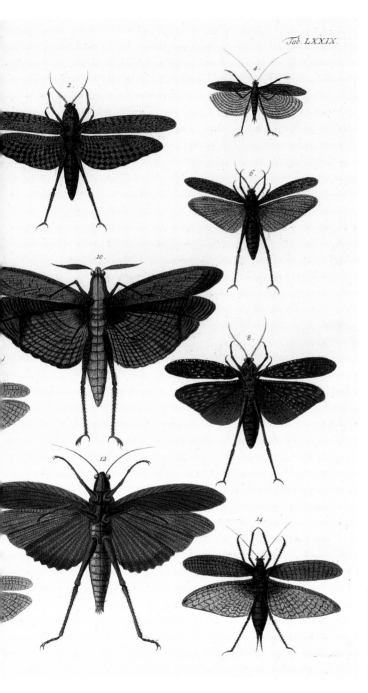

Tab. LXXIX.

Grasshoppers and
katydids · Feld- und
Laubheuschrecken ·
Criquets et sauterelles ·
Saltamontes y langostas
7–8 Bush locusts ·
Wanderheuschrecken ·
Sauterelles · Langostas
migratorias

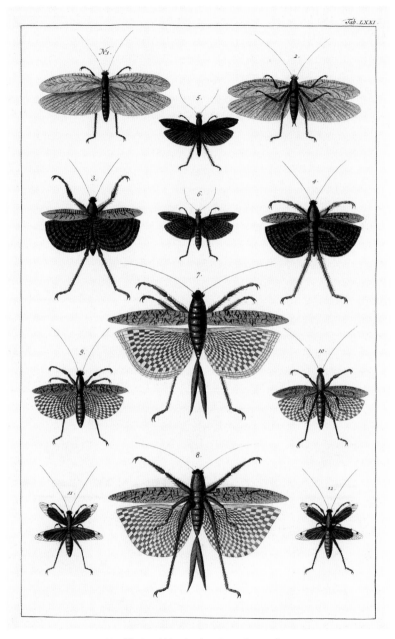

Tab. LXXI

Katydids · Langfühlerschrecken · Sauterelles · Ensíferas

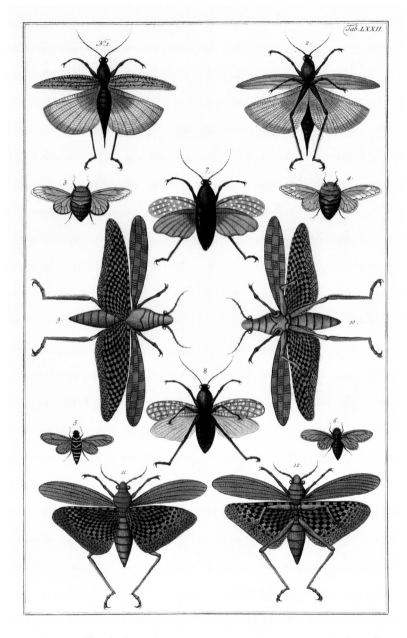

Tab. LXXII.

1–2, 9–12 Grasshoppers · Feldheuschrecken · Orthoptères · Ortópteros **3–8** Hemipterans · Wanzen · Hémiptères · Hemípteros
11–12 Grasshoppers · Feldheuschrecken · Criquets géants à ailes rouges · Ortópteros

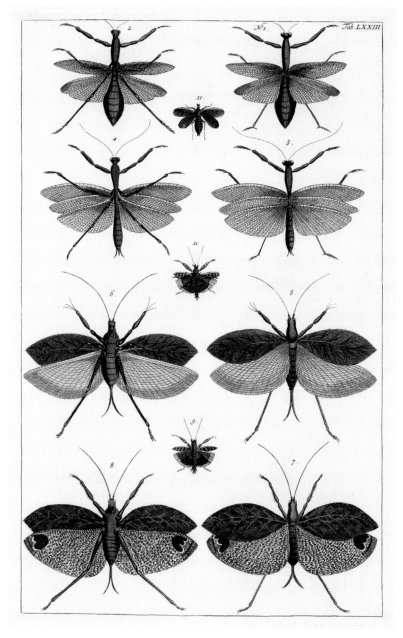

1–4, 9–10 Praying mantids · Gottesanbeterinnen · Mantes · Mantis religiosas
5–8 Katydids · Langfühlerschrecken · Sauterelles · Ensíferas **11** Bug · Wanze · Punaise · Hemíptero

Tab. LXXIV.

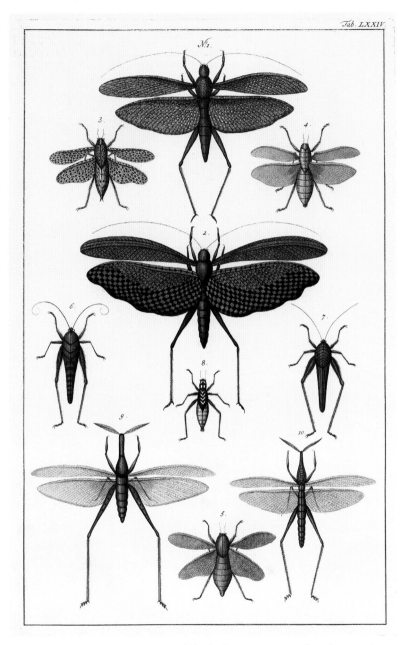

Grasshoppers, crickets and katydids · Lang- und Kurzfühlerschrecken · Criquets et sauterelles · Saltamontes y langostas

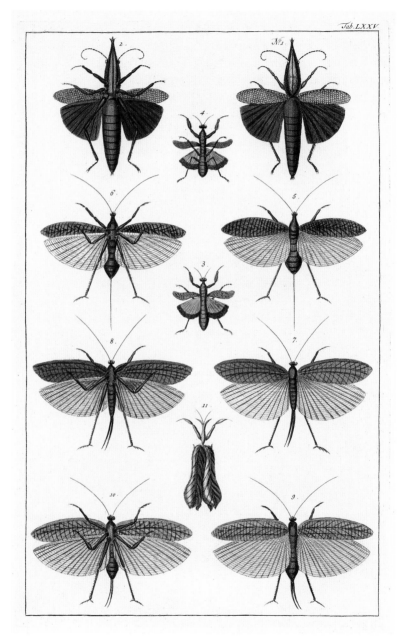

Tab. LXXV

1–2 Grasshoppers · Kurzfühlerschrecken · Criquets · Saltamontes **3–4, 11** Praying mantids · Gottesanbeterinnen · Mantes · Mantis religiosas **5–10** Katydids · Langfühlerschrecken · Sauterelles · Ensíferas

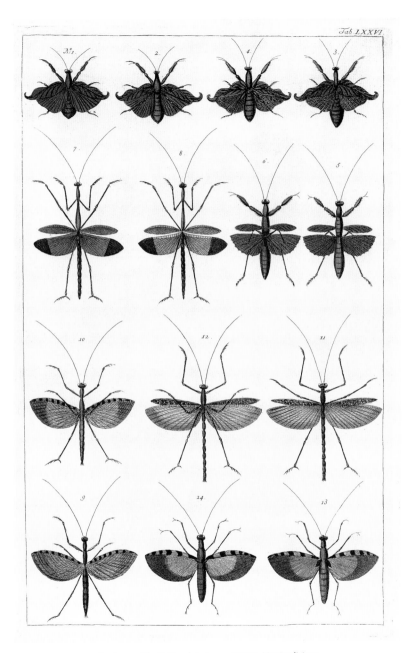

Praying mantids · Gottesanbeterinnen · Mantes · Mantis religiosas

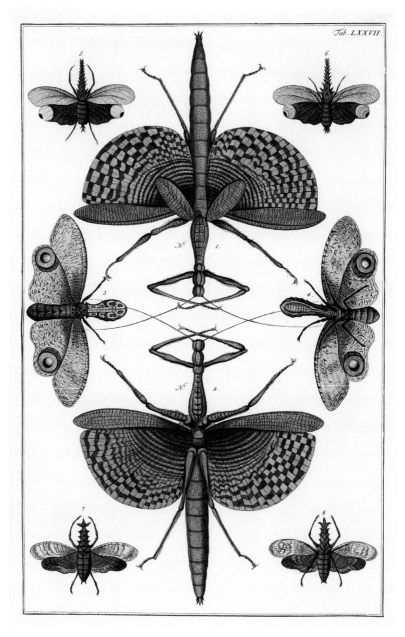

1–2 Walking stick · Stabheuschrecke · Grand phasme ailé · Sipyloidea sipylus 3–4 Greater lanternfly · Großer Laternenträger ·
Fulgore porte-lanterne · Pyrops candelarius 5–8 Cicadas · Zikaden · Homoptères · Cigarra

Tab. LXXVIII.

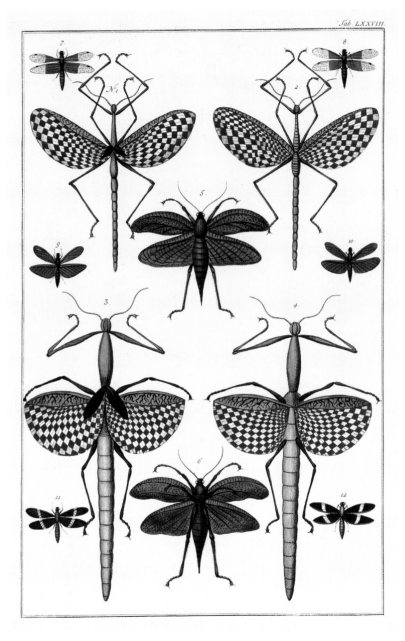

1–4 Walking stick · Stabheuschrecken · Phasmes · Sipyloidea sipylus
5–6 Katydids · Langfühlerschrecken · Sauterelles · Ensíferas **7–12** Dragonflies · Libellen · Libellules · Libélulas

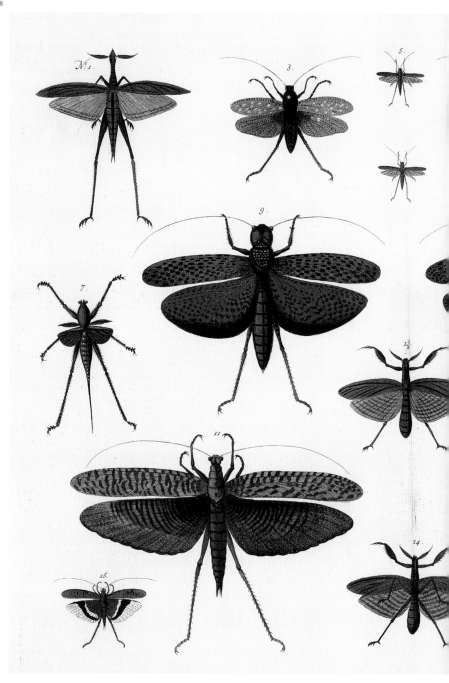

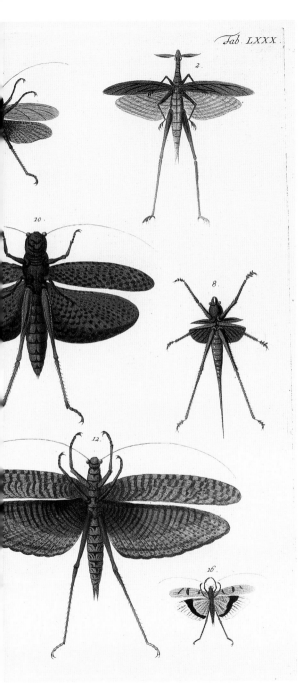

Tab. LXXX.

1–12, 15–16 Grasshoppers and katydids ·
Feld- und Laubheuschrecken ·
Criquets et sauterelles · Langostas
y saltamontes **1–2** Mediterranean
grasshoppers · Heuschrecken ·
Criquets · Langostas mediterráneas
13–14 Praying mantids · Gottesanbeterinnen · Mantes · Mantis religiosas

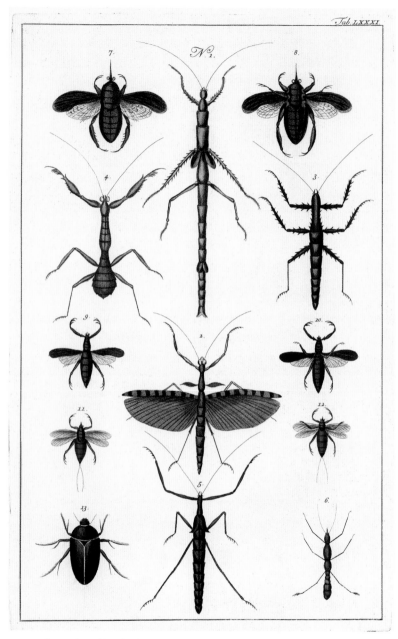

Tab. LXXXI

1, 3, 5–6 Walking sticks · Stabheuschrecken · Phasmes · Sipyloidea sipylus **2, 4** Praying mantids · Gottesanbeterinnen · Mantes · Mantis religiosas **7–12** Water bugs · Wasserwanzen · Punaises aquatiques · Chinches acuáticas **13** Water beetle · Wasserkäfer · Coléoptère aquatique · Coleóptero acuático

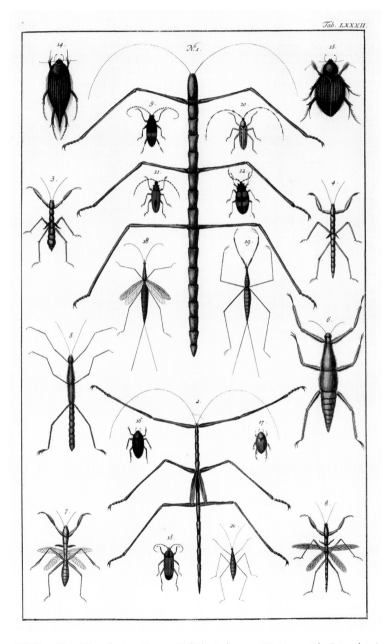

1, 2, 5–6 Walking sticks · Stabheuschrecken · Phasmes · Sipyloidea sipylus 3–4, 7–8 Praying mantids · Gottesanbeterinnen ·
Mantes · Mantis religiosas 9–17 Beetles · Käfer · Coléoptères · Coleópteros 18–20 Bugs · Wanzen · Punaises · Hemípteros

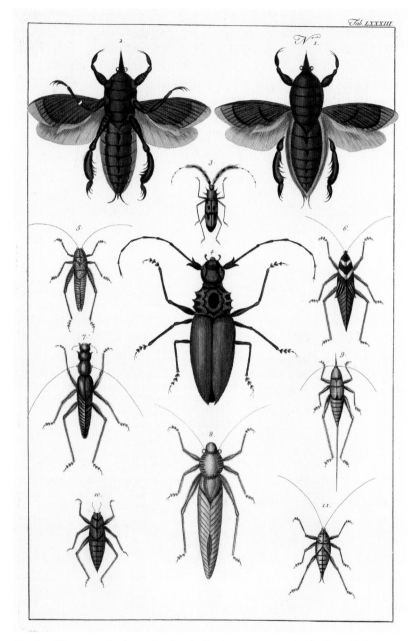

Tab. LXXXIII.

1–2 Water bug · Wasserwanze · Punaise aquatique (Nèpe) · Chinche acuática **3–4** Longhorn beetle · Bockkäfer · Longicorne · Cerambycidae **5–11** Grasshoppers and katydids · Heuschrecken · Criquets et sauterelles · Saltamontes y langostas

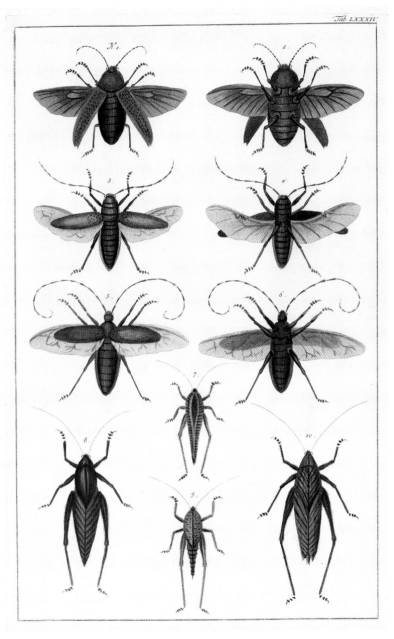

Tab. LXXXIV

1–6 Beetles · Käfer · Coléoptères · Coleópteros **7–10** Grasshoppers and katydids · Heuschrecken · Orthoptères · Ortópteros

1–12 Cicadas · Zikaden · Cigales · Cigarras **5–6** Manniferous cicadas · Mannazikaden/Eschenzikaden · Cigales de l'orne ·
Cicada sinuatipennis **13–20** Cockroaches · Schaben · Blattes · Cucarachas **17–18** Brazilian cockroaches · Brasilianische Schaben ·
Blattes brésiliennes · Cucarachas brasileñas **21–22** Jewel beetles · Prachtkäfer · Buprestes · Buprestidae

Tab. LXXXVI.

1, 3 Damselflies · Wasserjungfern · Demoiselles · Zygóptera 2 Lacewing · Netzflügler · Ascalaphe · Planipennia
4, 6, 9, 11, 14–16, 19, 21 Dragonflies · Libellen · Libellules · Libélulas 5, 12–13, 17–18 Ant lions · Ameisenlöwen ·
Fourmislions · Hormigas león 7–8 Dragonflies · Großlibellen · Libellules · Libélulas
10 Neuropterans · Netzflügler · Planipenne · Planipennia 22 Butterfly · Schmetterling · Papillon · Mariposa

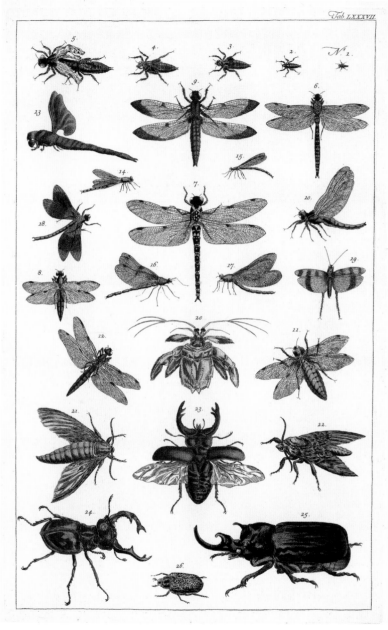

Tab. LXXXVII.

1–18 Dragonflies · Libellen · Libellules · Libélulas 19 Grasshopper · Feldheuschrecke · Criquet · Saltamontes
20 Crustacean · Krebs · Crustacé · Crustáceos 21, 22 Hawkmoths · Schwärmer · Sphinx · Esfinges 23–24 Stag beetles ·
Hirschkäfer · Lucanes cerfs-volants · Ciervo volante 25 Hercules beetle · Herculeskäfer · Dynaste hercule ·
Dynastes hércules 26 May beetle · Maikäfer · Hanneton · Abejorro

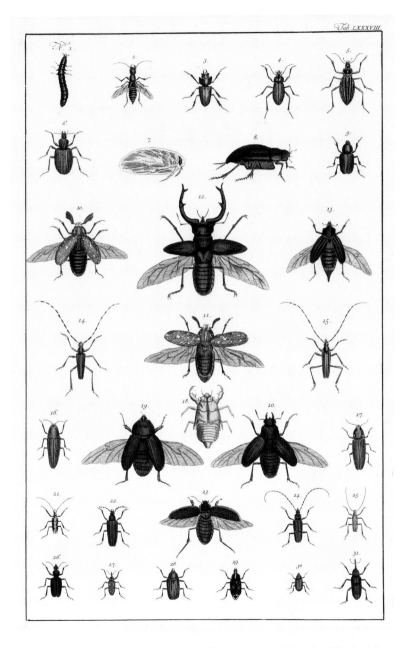

1, 3–4, 8, 21, 25–26, 29–30 Beetles · Käfer · Coléoptères · Coleótero 2 Rove beetle · Kurzflügelkäfer · Staphylin ·
Staphylinidae 5–6 Carabids/Ground beetles · Laufkäfer · Carabidés · Carabidae 9–11, 13, 18–20, 23, 28 Cockchafers ·
Blatthornkäfer · Scarabées · Escarabeos 14–15, 22 Longhorn beetles · Bockkäfer · Longicornes · Cerambycidae
16–17 Click beetles · Schnellkäfer · Taupins · Elateridae 27, 31 Weevils · Rüsselkäfer · Charançons · Curculionidae

Tab. LXXXIX

1–2 Water-beetles · Wasserkäfer · Hydrophiles · Hydrophildae 3–4 Mole criquets · Maulwurfsgrillen · Courtilières ·
Gryllotalpidae 5–8 Stag beetles · Hirschkäfer · Lucanes cerfs-volants · Ciervos volantes 9–21 Cockchafers ·
Blatthornkäfer · Scarabées · Escarabeos 22 Wedge-shaped beetle · Fächerkäfer · Rhipiphoridé · Rhipiphoridae

Tab. XCI.

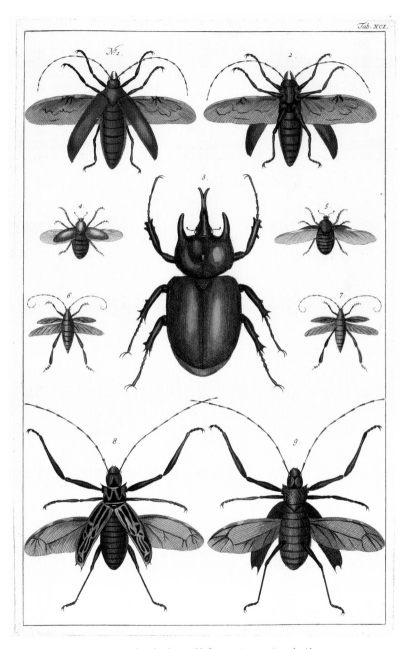

1–2, 8–9 Longhorn beetles · Bockkäfer · Longicornes · Cerambycidae
3 Cockchafer · Blatthornkäfer · Scarabée · Escarabeos 4–5 Beetles · Käfer · Coléoptères · Coleópteros

Tab. XC.

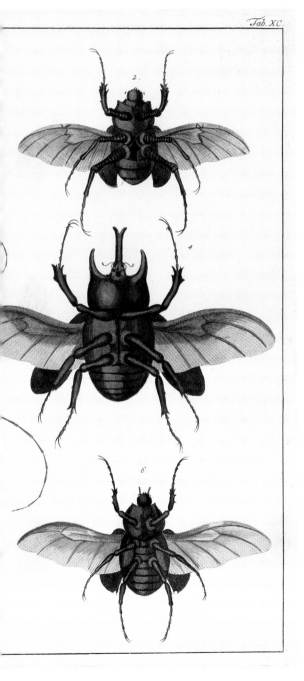

1–6 Cockchafers · Blatthornkäfer ·
Scarabées · Escarabeos
7–9 Longhorn beetles · Bockkäfer ·
Longicornes · Cerambycidae

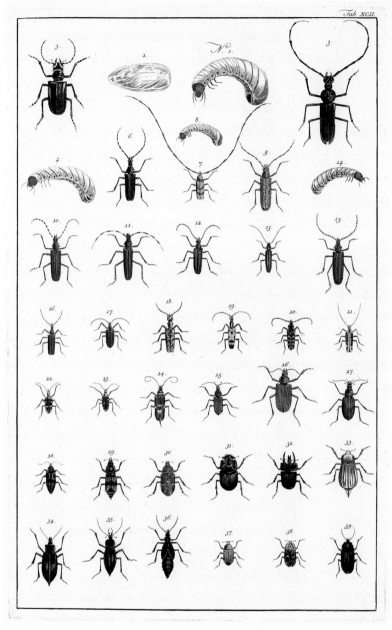

Tab. XCII.

1–2, 4, 8, 14, 31 Cockchafers · Blatthornkäfer · Scarabées · Escarabeos 3, 6–7, 9–13, 15–24 Longhorn beetles · Bockkäfer · Longicornes · Cerambycidae 25–27 Carabids/Ground beetles · Laufkäfer · Carabidés · Carabidae 28–30, 33–35, 37–39 Carrion beetles · Aaskäfer · Silphidés · Silphidae 32 Dor beetle · Mistkäfer · Géotrupidé · Geotrupidae 36 Blister beetle · Ölkäfer · Méloé · Meloidae

Tab. XCIII.

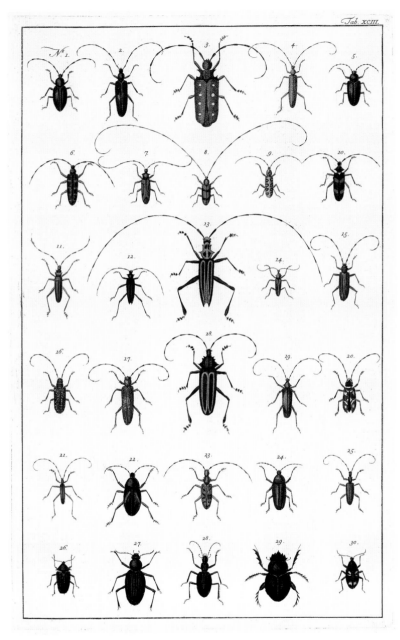

1–25 Longhorn beetles · Bockkäfer · Longicornes · Cerambycidae 26 Carabid/Ground beetle · Laufkäfer ·
Carabidé · Carabidae 27–28 Black beetles · Schwarzkäfer · Ténébrionidés · Tenebrionidae 29 Cockchafer ·
Blatthornkäfer · Scarabée · Escarabeo 30 Carrion beetle · Aaskäfer · Silphidé · Silphidae

124

Tab. XCIV.

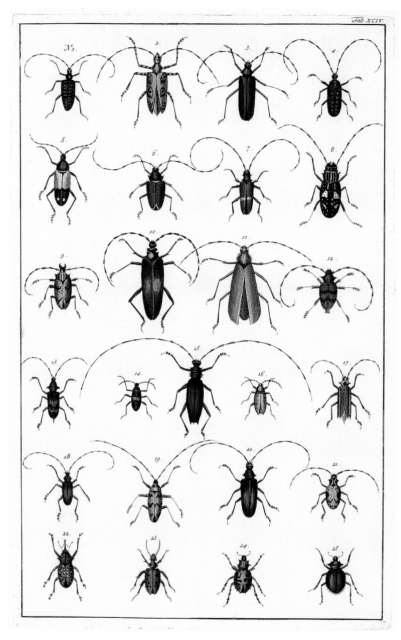

1–13, 15, 17–21 Longhorn beetles · Bockkäfer · Longicornes · Cerambycidae **14–16** Beetles · Käfer · Coléoptères · Coleópteros
22 Weevil · Rüsselkäfer · Charançon · Curculionidae **23** Leaf beetle · Schilfkäfer · Chrysomèle (Donacie) · Donaciinae

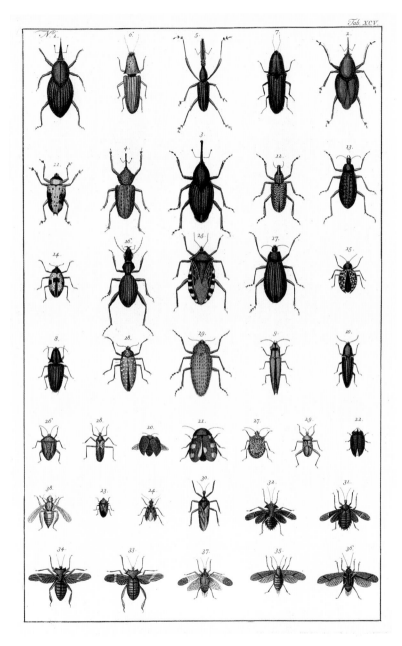

1–5, 12 Weevils · Rüsselkäfer · Charançons · Curculionidae 6–10 Click beetles · Schnellkäfer · Taupins · Elateridae
13, 16–17 Carabids/Ground beetles · Laufkäfer · Carabidés · Carabidae 14–15, 20–21 Leaf beetles · Blattkäfer · Chrysomèles ·
Chrysomelidae 18–19 Jewel beetles · Prachtkäfer · Buprestes · Buprestidae 24 Tiger beetle · Sandlaufkäfer ·
Cicindèle · Cincidela 38 Aculeate hymenopterans · Stechimme · Aculéates · Aculeate

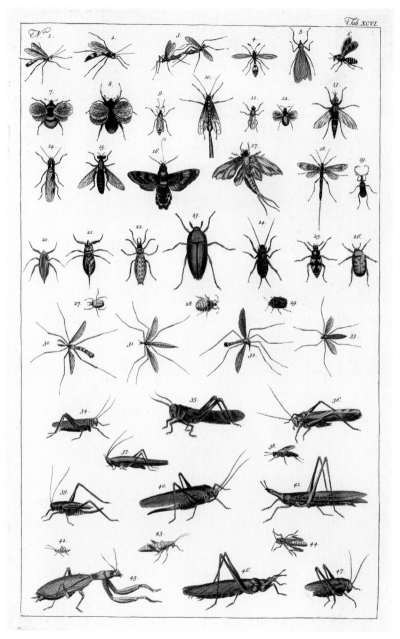

1–2, 4, 6–10, 12, 18, 38 Hymenopterans · Hautflügler · Hyménoptères · Himenópteros 3, 11, 13, 15, 30–33 Flies · Fliegen · Diptères · Dípteros 14 Stonefly · Steinfliege · Plécoptère · Plecópteros 19, 22–23, 25–27 Beetles · Käfer · Coléoptères · Coleópteros 28, 29 Bugs · Wanzen · Punaises · Hemíptero 34–37, 39–44, 46, 47 Grasshoppers and katydids · Heuschrecken · Criquets et sauterelles · Langostas y saltamontes 45 Praying mantid · Gottesanbeterin · Mante · Mantis religiosa

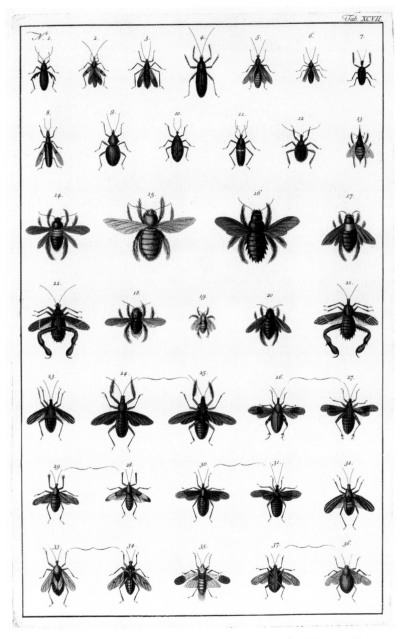

Tab. XCVII.

1–2, 12–13, 21–35 Bugs · Wanzen · Punaises · Hemípteros **4, 7–11, 36, 37** Beetles · Käfer · Coléoptères · Coleópteros
5–6 Hymenopterans · Hautflügler · Hyménoptères · Himenópteros **14–20** Bees · Bienen · Apoïdés · Abejas

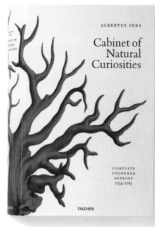

Albertus Seba
Cabinet of Natural Curiosities
Irmgard Müsch, Jes Rust, Rainer Willmann /
Hardcover, 636 pp. /
€ 200 / $ 200 / £ 135 / ¥ 25.000

"This is a massive book. It is also, probably, one of the most beautiful you are ever likely to see." —*Fortean Times*, London

"Buy them all and add some pleasure to your life."

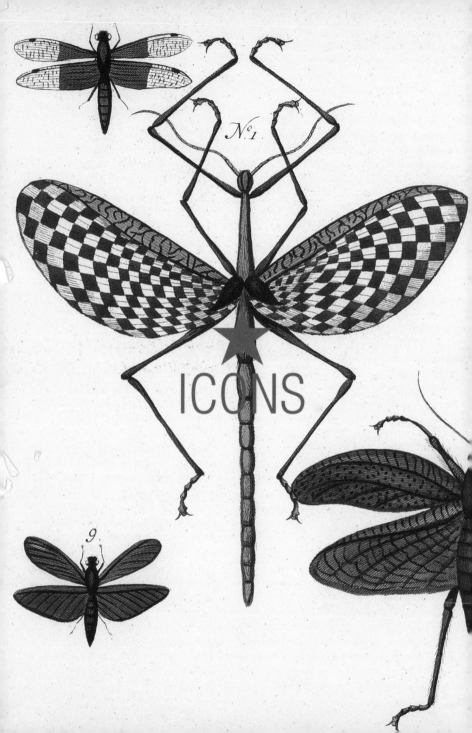

N.º 1.

9.